THE TROUBLE WITH faking

Also by Rochelle Morgan

THE TROUBLE SERIES

The Trouble with Flying

The Trouble with Flirting

The Trouble with Faking

The Trouble with Falling

THE TROUBLE WITH faking

ROCHELLE MORGAN

The Trouble with Faking
By Rachel Morgan writing as Rochelle Morgan

First published in 2014. This edition 2017.

ISBN 978-0-9947040-4-7

I'VE BEEN IN LOVE WITH THE BOY NEXT DOOR SINCE I WAS ten. It's a cliché, I know, but I couldn't help it. His family moved into the house next door to ours one sweltering day in January, and I couldn't take my eyes off the sandy haired boy. Even at twelve, he was handsome.

I sat in the shade in the front garden, pretending to read my book while catching glimpses of him and his parents through the fence. It took me the whole day to work up the courage, but as evening drew closer and the temperature changed from oppressive to almost bearable, I walked next door, introduced myself, and invited him over for a swim. Having an excellent view of their garden from my upstairs bedroom window, I was all too familiar with the current algae-infested state of their swimming pool. And on a day as hot as that one, he couldn't say no to an invitation like mine, could he?

He didn't. Damien Sanders accepted my invitation, and we've been friends ever since.

Which sucks, of course, because of the part where I'm in love with him.

"Andi, who are you staring at?"

"Hmm? What? I'm not staring." I tear my gaze from the other side of the vast dining hall where Damien just walked in with two guys. It's been three days since I moved into my new home—Fuller Hall, Upper Campus, UCT—and I haven't spoken to him yet. I've been busy with orientation stuff, and every time I've had a free moment, Damien hasn't been available. I guess being a sub-warden at Smuts has kept him busy too.

Smuts Hall. The guys' residence across the parking lot. That's right. After two years apart, Damien is once again The Boy Next Door.

"You're definitely staring at someone," Carmen says as my eyes wander over her shoulder once more. She twists around just as Mike—a guy we met during the awkward Fuller-Smuts icebreaker thing on our first night here—looks over and waves at us. Carmen returns the wave, then looks back at me with a giggle. "Was it him you were checking out?"

"Ha! No." I take a bite of my burger to avoid elaborating.

"Maybe you *should* be checking him out," she says, twisting a strand of dark hair around her finger. "Unless," she adds, eyeing the *I ♥ Mr Darcy* badge pinned to my T-shirt with a grin, "book boyfriends are enough for you?"

I roll my eyes at her. "Maybe *you* should check him out."

"Well, you know, I would, but guys tend to feel intimidated by me."

I laugh and nod. My newest friend is taller than almost every guy in this room, and probably smarter too. I can see how guys might find that intimidating.

"Besides, he's too white for me," she adds. "Too preppy. Too … European."

"Hmm. So you want a coloured guy?" I can understand that. I've somehow never found myself attracted to someone who isn't my own race, so maybe it's the same for her. Actually, scratch that. I've never found myself attracted to someone who isn't Damien.

"Maybe," she says. "That would certainly make my grandma happy." A sachet of salt smacks her cheek before landing on her plate. She snaps her head to the side and glares at the table beside ours where a bunch of guys are doubled over with laughter. "Hey, watch it!" she yells. She grabs the salt sachet and chucks it at the guy with the spoon in his hand—the one who obviously flicked the sachet in the first place.

"So, not *that* coloured guy," I say, trying to suppress a laugh.

"Definitely not. Eish, why do these guys have to share our dining hall with us? Don't they have their own?"

I shrug. "They do. I don't know why they don't use it." I finish off the last two bites of my burger and look around for Damien. He's gone. Before I can think about it, I'm on my feet. "I need to go talk to someone quickly," I tell Carmen. "I'll be back in a few minutes."

"I'll be in my room," she says, standing with her tray in her hands. "Don't forget the treasure hunt thing."

"Yeah, yeah." I get rid of my tray, then hurry out of the dining hall. Damien's probably on sub-warden duty or something, and in fifteen minutes I have to be back in Fuller's upper common room with the rest of the freshers to start some silly treasure hunt, but I can't let another night pass without at least saying hi to him. I run along the corridor and out of reception. I scan the parking lot between Fuller and Smuts, but I don't see him. Maybe he never left. Maybe he's visiting what's-her-name, his g—

"Hey, Andi!" I look to my left and see Damien standing in the road behind Fuller. He waves, and I run the short distance towards him. I crash into him with a hug, and he winds his arms around me, wrapping me in his deliciously familiar woody, citrusy scent. He isn't too tall or too short. Not too built or too skinny or too squishy. He's perfection wrapped around me. "I've missed you," he says. "You and your quirky dress sense." He steps back and smiles down at my pink polka-dot T-shirt and lime green suspenders. The *I ♥ Mr Darcy* badge is pinned directly over a large white polka dot.

"Well, my quirky dress sense and I have missed you too," I say with a laugh, tucking loose strands of orange-red hair behind my ear.

"I've been wondering when I'd finally see you. They've

been keeping you busy with O-Week stuff?"

"Yes." I push my hands into my back shorts pockets. "Faculty orientation during the day, and then res stuff in the evenings. That icebreaker with Smuts, a social with Kopano, high tea with Baxter, and a treasure hunt tonight."

"They haven't forced you to hike up a mountain yet?" he asks with a grin. He's well aware of how terrified I am of heights.

I groan. "That's coming up on Saturday. Anyway." I remove one hand from a pocket and touch his arm, because I'm ridiculous and I can't help myself. "What are you doing out here in the road?"

"Oh, just searching for a flash drive. It was in my pocket earlier, and now it's gone. I thought it might have fallen out when I was walking along here earlier."

"Oh. Sorry. I hope it didn't have anything too important on it." I look around, hoping I might spot the missing flash drive.

"No, not really. I think I've pretty much given up on finding it now. Anyway, you've got to get back for your treasure hunt, but once O-Week is over, we must catch up. Just come over to Smuts when you're free and ask the receptionist to call me."

"Sure." I smile as happiness heats up my insides. I know it's stupid. I know he only thinks of me as a good friend. But part of me always hopes that maybe *now* is the time he'll start thinking of me as … more. He pulls me into another hug, and my flyaway hair gets stuck in the chain around his neck. And then we're both laughing again as I try to pull it free, and I'm forcing myself not to think about his face being so close I can feel his breath on my cheek. I tug the strand of hair until it comes loose, then push it over my shoulder.

"Sorry about that," Damien says. He gives my arm a squeeze and adds, "Have fun tonight."

I nod, then turn back to Fuller. I'm just about floating as I head through the old wooden doors, but the sight that greets me in reception brings me firmly back to earth.

A girl with perfect brown curls tumbling over her shoulders, arms crossed over her chest, and eyes so furious they may as well be shooting poison watches me from the other side of reception. She steps away from her group of equally furious-looking friends and marches across the foyer towards me.

"Who. The Hell. Are you?"

"Hi," I say to the girl who looks like she wants to tear my eyes out. "You must be Charlotte. Damien's told me all about you." Not that I was interested in hearing anything about his latest girlfriend. "I'm Andi. Damien's friend."

"His *friend?* How about secret lover?"

I take a step back. "Excuse me?"

"I *know* he's been cheating on me. He's been paying less and less attention to me, and now I find him sneaking around the back of Fuller with his hands all over you."

"Um, I don't think that's what happened." Despite any wish I might have had to the contrary.

"I know what I saw, so don't even try to—"

"Charlotte," I say with as much patience as I can muster. "I am not his secret lover."

"Don't lie to me," she shouts. "My friend saw the two of you together last year."

"What? Oh, when I flew here for those two days in April? I was visiting my sister. Damien just picked me up from the airport."

"So it wasn't you he was sitting on mem stone with?"

"Mem stone?"

"That big block of stone in between Fuller and Smuts!" she yells.

"Oh. Yes, that was me. We chatted for a bit before he dropped me off at my sister's. You know, just two old friends catching up."

"Liar!" she shrieks. "I *know* he's been cheating on me."

"Listen up," I say, rapidly losing my patience. "I have a *big* problem with cheating, and there's no way I'd ever be involved in it in *any* way. Damien and I have been friends for eight years, and if that bothers you, you need to get over it."

I step past her and her friends and swipe my card to get from reception into the rest of the building. I stomp all the way to F flat before looking at my watch and realising I'm late for the treasure hunt meeting. I turn and hurry back to the upper common room. I open the door and slip quietly inside, but I manage to earn myself several stern looks from a few House Comm members before seating my butt on the carpet beside Carmen.

I remove my phone from my pocket and type a message to Damien: **I met Charlotte. She's lovely. She also thinks you're cheating on her with me. You might want to have a chat with her.**

I put my phone away and pay attention to the treasure

hunt instructions. We're divided into several groups, and each group is given a different clue. We're all supposed to end up in the same place at the end, of course, but to avoid all groups simply following the lead group, no group will be able to get to the end in the same way. It feels a bit like something I'd be expected to do in primary school, and I'm starting to wonder if the rumours about Fuller being the boring res full of smart, nerdy girls is true. I'm also wondering if the fact that I'm enjoying the idea of this treasure hunt makes me boring and nerdy too.

Who cares?

I take the clue from Carmen and read it quickly. We shout out the answer at the same time—"The bench in reception!"—ignore the few members of our group who roll their eyes at our enthusiasm, and head downstairs, chatting along with everyone else who appears to find this fun.

After hunting down five different clues, we eventually find a folded-up paper labelled 'Last Clue' that points us in the direction of Rugby Road in front of Smuts. We head outside, passing a group of girls retrieving a note stuck to the warden's car and another group of girls huddled around the receptionist's window. They look at us, then start running. And whether this is officially a competition or not, we all want to be the first to get to the end, so we start running too. Past mem stone and down the steps. It would be enough to terrify any sane person, this hoard of girls giggling and shrieking as they run towards a parked car with a white X painted onto the windscreen.

Carmen reaches the car first and lets out a whoop of joy.

The rest of us crowd around her a second later. All the car windows are down, and we peer inside and find bags of marshmallows and slabs of chocolate covering the seats. A sign stuck to the steering wheel says 'Hot Chocolate on Jammie Steps at 8:30 pm.'

One person says, "Yum," a second person says, "Really? Is that it?" and a third person suggests we grab all the chocolate and run before the rest of the girls get here.

Then I hear a shout from above us. I look up. Leaning out of a row of Smuts windows are a whole lot of freshmen with brightly coloured balloons in their hands. Another shout, and they all let go.

Shrieks erupt as water bombs hit the car, the road, and the pavement, exploding all over us. We run back up the road with bursting water bombs chasing us all the way. We reach the front door, and I lean against the wall, shaking with silent laughter. My hair and T-shirt are soaked from the balloon that hit my back as I ran, and the girls who hadn't yet made it to the end of the treasure hunt stare at us from the doorway. One asks, "Do we have to do that too?"

I laugh even harder as Carmen says, "I don't think so. I'm pretty sure the water bombs weren't part of the treasure hunt plan."

"They most certainly were not," one of our House Comm members says, pushing through the crowd of girls and marching towards Smuts. She doesn't have to go far, though, because two guys from the Smuts House Comm are halfway across the parking lot, their hands already raised in surrender—although their cheeky grins suggest they're not exactly sorry about the water bombing. She begins yelling at them about sabotaging her perfectly planned treasure hunt, and they argue that the treasure hunt was lame, and they were only trying to liven things up.

I twist my hair over my shoulder and squeeze the water from it. "I think I enjoyed being attacked by water bombs," I say to Carmen. "How about you?"

"Eish, my hair's gonna frizz out on me now, but aside from that, yeah. It was fun. The best part, though, is that we're now completely within our rights to retaliate."

"Oh yes. You're right. Any ideas?"

"We should put evil clown masks on and hide in their rooms and jump out after they've gone to bed."

I blink at her. "You're a little bit scary, you know that?"

"I've been told."

"Please remind me never to get on your bad side, because I don't think—"

"Hey, Andi?"

I look up to find Damien walking out of Fuller. "Oh, hi." I twist some more water out of my hair and glance around to see if Charlotte's anywhere nearby ready to attack me. "Did you get my message?"

"Yes. We need to talk."

MOST STUDENTS IN SMUTS HAVE ONE ROOM TO THEM-selves—or half a room, if they're unlucky enough to be sharing with someone—but as a sub-warden, Damien gets both a bedroom and a living room. His living room has a couch, a desk, a bar fridge, and a bookcase with a bicycle leaning against it and a kettle and microwave on top. Quite bare, according to my tastes, but I tend to like—as my mother calls it—an 'overcrowded' room.

"Uh, just make yourself at home," Damien says, gesturing to the couch. "I'll get you a towel."

"Thanks." I notice a frame on his desk housing a picture of him and Charlotte. I turn my back on it and walk to the window. No city-facing view for Damien. He gets to see the inside quad of Smuts. Below me, a guy and girl sit on the grass chatting.

"Here you go," Damien says, tossing a towel to me.

I run it over my hair a few times before wrapping it around my shoulders and sitting down. "So did you talk to Charlotte?"

He sits on the other end of the couch with a sigh. "She broke up with me."

"What?" I struggle with the two conflicting emotions coursing through me. Half of me grieves to know that someone I care about is hurting, while the other half rejoices that he no longer has a girlfriend. "I'm so sorry. I tried to tell her there was nothing going on—"

"It's fine. Don't worry about it. It's actually a relief."

"A relief?"

He nods. "I started to realise we're not really right for each other. I spent the holidays trying to figure out what to say and how best to end it—you know, without hurting her too much—but I guess she got there before me."

"I guess," I say slowly. I certainly didn't see this coming. I thought I'd probably be spending my university years the same way I spent my high school years: watching Damien with someone else.

"I mean, I obviously told her I wasn't cheating on her," he adds, "but she seemed intent on believing her own story."

"Weird. How did the two of you end up dating if she isn't really your type?"

"I suppose I didn't know her that well." He scratches his neck. "She's hard-working, takes her studies seriously, but she's also fun to be with, and I liked that about her. But I didn't realise back then that she has a tendency to overdramatise things. It's exhausting the way she overreacts to everything. And she gossips a lot." He frowns. "And not in a nice way. It kinda made me feel guilty, listening to all the things she'd say about people. Especially when she kept expecting me to agree with her. Anyway. Sorry." He shakes his head and looks up at me. "Enough about Charlotte. What about you? I haven't seen you since … April last year? Is that when you found out about your dad and flew here to meet Livi?"

"Yes."

"So how's everything going? Are things okay with you and your mom now?"

Anger that wasn't there a moment ago flashes to the surface. I push it down. "You know, I'd rather not talk about my mother."

"Okay. Uh, are you still doing that blogging thing?"

I slide my lime green ballet pumps off so I can tuck my legs beneath me. "Vlogging. And yes, I'm still doing that."

"And the crafts?"

"Still doing that too."

"Awesome. I wish I were as passionate about stuff as you are. I watch your videos sometimes, you know."

I groan and cover my face with my hands. It's fine if thousands of other people watch my videos, but for some reason it's embarrassing to think of Damien watching them. Probably because I care way too much about his opinion.

"Hey, don't be silly," he says with a laugh. "Your videos rock. I love them." I drop my hands as he stands. "Do you want something to drink?" he asks. "Some coffee?"

"Only if you've got the good stuff."

He chuckles and turns the kettle on. "Still a coffee snob, huh?"

"Always have been, always will be."

"Sorry, I can't help you out then. Cape Town does have some amazing coffee shops, though. I can take you to some of them if you want."

"I'd love that." If it's as close as I'm going to get to a date with Damien, I'll take it.

He spoons coffee powder into a mug, then looks up at the sound of a knock on his door. He crosses the room and pulls the door open. Standing there is Mike, the guy who waved at us earlier in the dining hall.

"Hey, um, sorry. Oh, hi, Andi." He leans into the room to greet me. "Um, yeah." He gives Damien an apologetic look. "I sort of locked myself out of my room again."

"Sorry, man, I'm not on duty tonight," Damien says, not unkindly. "Go to reception, and they'll call the right person. He'll have to get the bolt cutter."

"Right, thanks. Sorry to bother you guys."

Damien shuts the door and turns to me. "I've already had to cut three locks since everyone moved in. And I'm one of four sub-wardens. I don't know how many the other guys have cut. Why can't people just keep their keys on them instead of leaving them inside their rooms?"

I hold up my lanyard and show him the student card and room keys dangling from the end. "I find it works pretty well to hang them around my neck."

"For you and most other students. Why can't everyone do that?"

"I don't know. Maybe Smutsmen are too cool for that."

He shakes his head, then pours boiling water into his mug. "Would you like water?" he asks, setting the kettle down. "I'm afraid that's the only other thing I can offer you. Or milk."

"Don't worry, I'm fine." I run my finger over a seam on the couch. "So how are your parents?"

"Oh, they're great." Damien returns to the couch with his hands wrapped around his coffee mug, which reminds me that I'm missing the hot chocolate gathering on Jammie steps—if it's still happening. I'd far rather be on Damien's couch, though. "It's only been a year since they left Joburg," he continues, "but they've settled into Simon's Town quickly and seem to be loving life there."

"Cool. Do you see them often?"

"Every few weekends, I guess. It's about forty-five minutes from here. In good traffic." A ping sounds from Damien's desk, and he gets up to fetch his phone. "Oh, great," he says after looking at the screen. "A message from Charlotte's cousin calling me a whole bunch of names I'd rather not say out loud."

"Lovely."

"Yeah." He sits and drops the phone onto the couch between us. He tilts his head back against the wall and sighs. "Hey, can I tell you something?"

"Sure. Anything."

"There's actually this girl I really like."

I sigh internally. Here it is. The reason I've never told Damien how I feel about him. And that reason is this: I know with complete certainty he doesn't feel the same way about me. He's told me about every girl he's ever liked, and I've never been on the list. "Okay," I say, trying my best to look interested.

"Her name's Marie. She's a third-year student in Fuller. Quieter than Charlotte, more my type. Back in first year, I tried to get to know her, but she didn't seem interested. I don't know, maybe I came across as too desperate," he says with a laugh. "So I gave up trying. Then in second year, after I started dating Charlotte, Marie started paying attention to me."

I chuckle. "That's bad timing."

"I know, but I think it was *because* I was dating Charlotte. As if being with someone else suddenly made her notice me."

"Because you weren't coming across as desperate anymore. Instead she saw you as *desirable*."

Damien laughs into his coffee mug. "Right. Yeah. Anyway, then Marie became the target of some of Charlotte's gossip—which was the cause of the first major fight Charlotte and I had—and Marie went back to ignoring me. But I've been thinking about her more and more lately."

"Well, now that you're single again, maybe it'll work out between the two of you." *Or maybe you'll finally notice* me.

"Maybe," he says. "I guess we'll see." He puts his coffee mug on the floor, while I lean back against the couch and arrange myself into a slightly more seductive pose—as seductive as one can be while wrapped in a towel. When his eyes are on me once more, I give him a smile that's meant to be alluring. He opens his mouth to say something, but he either changes his mind or forgets his words. He watches me with those beautiful blue-grey eyes, and maybe it's just my silly, wishful heart, but it feels like there's something different about—

A loud knock on the door ruins the moment. Because there was a moment. THERE WAS DEFINITELY A MOMENT.

"Damien, you in there?" comes a voice from the other side of the door.

Damien jumps up. "Yashen," he says as he opens the door. "Sorry, man, we were supposed to meet ten minutes ago. I just remembered."

"Hey, if you're busy," Yashen says, spotting me, "we can do it tomorrow evening."

"No, no, let's get it done. Andi, I'm so sorry." Damien turns to me. "I've got to organise this tutoring programme with Yashen."

"Oh, no problem." I get to my feet and hang the damp towel over the back of the desk chair. "I'm sure there's some O-Week activity I'm supposed to be doing now." Even though I'd like nothing more than to get back to THAT MOMENT.

"Cool. I'll walk you out," Damien says. "I'll be there in a minute, Yashen."

"Okay. Oh, and we're meeting in Paul's room, not mine."

Damien nods, and the impossibly skinny Yashen runs down the stairs while Damien locks his door. We manage to say nothing as we walk back to reception, which is weird for us, because we've always had things to talk about. We stand by the front door of Smuts, he thanks me for visiting, I thank him for the towel, and then as we lean in to hug one another, his lips brush over my cheek.

HE KISSED MY CHEEK.

And then he's looking at me awkwardly and mumbling goodbye and hurrying away before I can say a word. And I'm left feeling like I'm floating once more, because Damien Sanders has FINALLY NOTICED ME!

4

I'M TORN FROM A DREAM IN WHICH DAMIEN IS MY TUTOR by a blaring siren. I sit up and blink at the darkness as my brain struggles to catch up with my body.

Night time.

My bedroom.

Siren.

Running footsteps.

That means …

Fire drill?

I rub my eyes and groan as a memory of House Comm members warning us of the possibility of an upcoming fire drill surfaces. Someone pounds on my door, and I almost fall out of bed in fright. "Andi, hurry up," Carmen shouts. "You don't get to sleep through this."

I stumble out of bed, trip over a box of pin badges, and fall against my desk. I feel across the desk surface for my lamp switch before I manage to do myself any more harm. Once the lamp is on, I grab my keys and a hoodie and slide my feet into my slippers. "I'm here, I'm here," I mumble as I open my door.

Carmen and I join the mass of sleepy-eyed, pyjama-clad Fullerites shuffling towards the emergency exit. We congregate on the grass outside Fuller's aged walls. "Over here," our flat rep calls to us, and we huddle with the rest of F flat. I close my eyes and try not to sway. I wonder if it's possible to fall asleep while standing.

"Andi, you okay?" Carmen asks.

"Mmm." It feels like too much effort to open my mouth and add more words. Words like, *I don't handle sleep interruptions particularly well.*

"Do they check our rooms?" someone whispers.

I crack my eyelids open so I can see who it is. A girl from E flat. Jane, Jamie, Jenny. Something like that.

"I don't know," her friend says. "Why?"

"Well hopefully they don't open any cupboards."

Her friend starts laughing. "Don't tell me. Brian never left, and you made him hide in the cupboard."

The first girl elbows her friend in the ribs. "What else was I supposed to do with him when the fire alarm went off?"

"How fortunate it wasn't a real fire," Carmen says loudly, and both girls glare at her.

I smile and let my eyelids fall closed again.

Eventually someone does a roll call, after which we all traipse back inside. "How often do we have to do this?" I mumble to Carmen as we reach our floor in F flat.

She unlocks the door opposite mine. "Once a quarter, I think?"

"Ugh. That's far too often." I push my door closed behind me and fall into bed without bothering to remove my hoodie. I switch off the lamp and snuggle beneath the duvet, hoping to spend my few remaining hours of sleep in another Damien dream.

After the fire drill in the early hours of Friday morning, a braai that finished way too late on Friday night, and a hike on Saturday morning that I was insane enough not to try and get out of, I feel as though I may collapse into a snoring heap at any moment. When Saturday evening arrives, I'm beyond relieved I'm not one of the girls getting ready to go out. I lean in the doorway of the room next to mine, which belongs to a girl named Kimmy, and watch her and Georgia, the other girl who lives on our floor, getting ready for the RAG Big Bash.

"I'm so glad I decided not to go," I tell them.

"Party pooper," Kimmy teases.

"That's me." I wave my hand in the air. "And I'm not the only one. I think there were quite a few girls who signed up for the Fuller movie night instead of the Big Bash."

"Yeah, all this O-Week stuff has been tiring," Georgia says, sitting on the edge of Kimmy's bed. "A simple movie night sounds pretty good right now."

"Hey, don't you dare abandon me," Kimmy says, pointing a mascara wand at Georgia.

"I won't. You know I don't want to miss out."

I check my phone, but there's still no message from Damien. I haven't heard a thing from him since the awkward cheek kiss. "Okay, well, have fun," I tell Kimmy and Georgia. "Movie's starting soon, so I've gotta go." I walk back to my room, change into some comfy clothes, grab two pillows, and head for the upper common room. I find it covered in mattresses, most of which are already occupied. I pick an empty one and make myself comfy. The lights are dim, the popcorn bowls are going around, and the movie is just beginning when Carmen sneaks in and sits down next to me.

"Yay, you're just in time," I tell her. "Have some popcorn."

"You—" she points her cell phone at me "—have some explaining to do."

"Me?" I sit up. "What did I do?"

"You didn't tell me the news."

"What news?"

"The news that a second-year Fullerite broke up with her boyfriend because he was cheating on her with you."

I roll my eyes. "That isn't *news*. It's a *rumour*, and it isn't true."

"Oh. Really?"

"Of course! You didn't—"

"Shh," the girl on the mattress next to ours says.

I lower my voice and continue. "You didn't really think I'd do something like that, did you?"

"Well, that's what I said to the first person who told me. But then I heard the same thing from two other people, so then I started to wonder."

"Oh, come on. This is—"

"Hey, I can't see," someone behind me says.

I lie down, tugging on Carmen's sleeve until she does the same. "How was your afternoon with your cousins?" I ask.

"Oh no," she whispers. "You don't get to change the subject that easily."

"What, I'm genuinely interested in how your—"

"It was fine. It's great hanging out with the cousins I've hardly seen over the past five years. Now why didn't you tell me about this silly rumour?"

"I don't know. I didn't tell anyone. I didn't realise it was being spread around as *news*."

"So there's no truth to it?"

"None at all. Damien and I are friends. That's it." I reach for my bag of M&Ms and open it. "We were neighbours until he left for university two years ago, and we've stayed friends since then. His girlfriend saw us hugging and totally overreacted."

"Okay." Carmen takes a handful of M&Ms. "I'm sorry if there might have been a moment when I doubted you."

"Don't worry about it. Just eat popcorn and chocolate and tell me how the movie ends, because I'm pretty sure I'll be asleep in about five minutes."

I settle back and focus on the TV screen. My eyelids

begin to droop almost immediately, but a vibration in my pocket gets my attention. I pull my phone out and read the message.

Damien: Hey. I'm on duty this evening so I can't leave Smuts. Do you want to visit if you're free after the movie thing?

Do I want to visit? Of course I want to visit. I force myself to put the phone down for a minute before replying so I don't seem SUPER desperate.

Andi: Sure. See you then :)

Carmen nudges me with her elbow. "What happened to being asleep in five minutes?"

I return the nudge. "What happened to it being rude to read other people's texts?"

"Ha! Andi, seriously. You should know by now that I have no problem with being rude."

"So, what does being on duty entail?" I ask Damien. "I mean, aside from having to be on site the entire time." I've been talking since the moment he came to reception to meet me. All I can think of is the awkward look he gave me the other night, and I'm worried that if I allow even a moment of silence between us, things will turn weird.

"Well, if anything goes wrong, I'm the one people call," Damien says as we climb the stairs to his room. "Basically, I'm the guy in charge tonight."

"Cool. It suits you, this job. You've always been the responsible type."

Damien smiles and unlocks his door. "Responsible doesn't equal boring, does it?"

"No, no, no. You're definitely not boring." I drop onto the couch and Damien closes the door.

Silent moment.

"So are you part of any clubs or societies?" I ask, rushing to fill the void. "I signed up for some stuff, but now I wonder if it might be too much."

"Okay, wait," Damien says, sitting on the desk chair and spinning it around to face me. "Before we talk about anything else, I need to apologise for the other night. There was definitely an awkward moment there, and I don't want it hanging between us because, you know, things have always been easy with us." He runs a hand over his short hair. "So … I'm sorry about the half-kiss thing. I *really* don't know what that was about. Seriously. I think I've had too many late nights recently, and I'm not functioning like a normal person. I apologise, and I hope you'll forgive me."

"I—yes, of course." The ember of hope inside me fizzles out. "Don't worry about it. Everything's cool." I try to convince myself that everything *is* cool. That this is fine. After all, I didn't honestly expect anything else, did I? "Hey, let's go sit on mem stone and watch the city lights," I say, feeling suddenly claustrophobic.

"Can't. Gotta stay here, remember?" He gives me an apologetic look.

"Oh yes. Sorry."

"Show me all the new things you've made since I moved to Cape Town," he says, removing his laptop from the desk and wheeling his chair across the room towards me. "I used to be up to date on every product in your store, but I think I've missed a lot over the past two years."

"Probably because I could no longer force you into helping me make them."

"I don't believe there was any forcing involved." He hands the laptop to me. "I'd deny it in front of my friends, of course, but I actually enjoyed helping you with *Alice in Wonderland* brooches and Mr Darcy button things and those pendants with the *Northmonger Abbey* quote."

"*Northanger Abbey*," I say with a laugh. "Anyway, this is the newest one." I lift my arm to show him the charm bracelet with five miniature classic novels attached to it.

"Cool. They look just like real books."

"That's the idea." I lift the lid of his laptop and find his Facebook page open. "Oh. Um, you have messages." I pass the laptop back to him, but not before I've seen some of the words in the little message windows open at the bottom of the page.

Damien sighs. "Great. I've now got people on Facebook letting me know I'm a cheat."

"Sorry about that." I bite my thumb nail. "And what about that girl Marie? Any luck with her?" WHY am I asking? I don't want to know about Damien's love life.

"No. Nothing. She's completely ignoring me." He closes Facebook and hands the laptop back to me.

"So I guess she's only interested in you when you're not available, huh?" I open a new browser window and type the Etsy address.

"Looks like it."

"You know," I say, sitting back as an idea slowly begins to form in my mind, "we could make it so that you're once again not available."

His eyebrows pinch together. "What do you mean?"

"We could …" *Don't say it, don't say it, don't say it.* "Pretend." *No, Andi, that is SUCH a bad idea. STOP TALKING NOW!* "We could pretend that we actually are together. We could act like the happiest, most in-love couple ever so that the girl you really like finally notices you, and the guy I really like finally notices me. Half of res already thinks there's something going on between us, so it would be entirely believable."

A hesitant smile plays on Damien's lips. "Wait. I can't figure out if you're joking or being serious."

I'm so surprised at myself for voicing this ridiculous idea that I start laughing. "I'm actually being serious. I mean, people do this in movies all the time. Why shouldn't we?" I ignore the internal voice reminding me that those are the kind of movies that annoy the heck out of me.

Damien narrows his eyes, but that half-smile is still there. "Don't the people in those movies generally end up falling for the people they're pretending to be with?"

"Well, yes," I admit, "but that's because those are movies. This is real life, and we both know exactly who we want. That will keep us focused."

"Wait, so … who is it that you want?"

You, I almost sigh out loud. But since I can't admit that, I grab the first name that comes to mind. "Mike. The first-year guy who was here the other evening."

"Mike? The guy who's barely been here a week and had to buy three padlocks already?"

"Okay, so he's a little forgetful when it comes to his room keys, but other than that he's great." That isn't a lie.

Mike *is* great. He sat with me on the hike near the end when it got too steep and all I could focus on was the sheer drop down the side of the mountain and my spinning head that made me want to fall over. "I really like him, but he seems to be interested in every other girl except me." Now that's a lie. I *don't* really like him, and he *doesn't* seem to be interested in every other girl. But if I can get Damien to fall for me at the end of all this, a few lies will be worth it.

"If he's interested in every other girl," Damien says, "maybe he isn't the right guy for you."

He isn't. You are. "Hey, do you like my idea or not?"

"I …" Damien chuckles to himself. "I think I actually do."

The dying embers inside me blaze to life. "So … are we really going to do this?"

Damien's eyes meet mine. "I think so. No, wait, wait. I don't want us to be known as the couple that got together behind Charlotte's back. We'll always have that cheating label, and that's horrible."

My heart sinks. "Yes, I guess you're right."

"But we can still do this. We just don't get together yet. We say we're still friends, and then, uh … the Valentine's Dance at the end of next week. Do you know about that?"

"Yes, I think I saw it on our calendar. It says we're having some kind of dinner thing with Smuts?"

"Yes. It's nothing fancy. Just a nice dinner and some pretty decor in the Fuller dining hall. It's for freshers, but sub-wardens are allowed to attend. We can let everyone see us dancing together there, and then officially start dating after that. And if anyone asks, we can say we've always been good friends—which is true—and when Charlotte accused us of secretly dating, we first laughed it off as a ludicrous idea, but the more we thought about it, the more we realised it was meant to be."

Well, at least that's all pretty much the truth from my side. "People probably won't believe you, though. They'll still think we got together before and you cheated on her."

He shrugs. "It's never bothered you what other people think, has it?"

"No. I'm just checking whether it bothers you."

He shakes his head. "No matter what the truth is, people will always think whatever they want to think."

"Okay. Great. So we'll find ways to be head-over-heels for each other in front of Marie and Mike, and that way they'll see what they're missing out on." Part of me is giddy at the thought that I'll finally get to hold and hug and kiss him the way I've always wanted to, while another part of me feels sick knowing Damien will just be pretending.

"Maybe we can try—"

A pounding on the door interrupts whatever plan Damien was about to suggest. The door opens before Damien can get there, and a well-built guy with a closely shaved head enters. "Dude, someone just fell out of a window into A quad."

"What?"

"Yip. Real idiot. I think his arm's broken."

Damien grabs his keys. "Disaster number one for the night. Andi, I'll be back just now."

He heads out while the other guy turns back to look at me. From this angle, I can see the decorative tattoo of a cross on his upper left arm. "Hey, you're Andi," he says. "Andi … Clark?"

"Um, yes." He must be a friend of Damien's if he knows who I am. "And you're the salt flicker," I add, realising I recognise him from the dining hall.

He raises an eyebrow. "The what?"

"You flicked a salt sachet at us the other night. You have pretty good aim, by the way. You hit my friend on the cheek."

"Oh, yes, I remember that. Tall, scary girl."

"That's the one."

"Well, no offence intended. We flick salt at everyone. And my official name is actually Noah Ferreira, not Salt Flicker."

"Right. Noah. Hey, you don't sound … I mean … nothing." I press my lips together as I realise I was probably about to say something inappropriate.

Noah frowns. "Sound what?"

"Nothing. Sorry. Sometimes I say things without thinking about them first. The words seem to bypass my internal filter. So … never mind."

He sits on Damien's wheeled desk chair and scoots closer. "Now you *have* to tell me."

I lean back on the couch "Fine. I was going to comment on your accent. It's … not what I expected."

"You mean because I'm a coloured guy living in the

Cape, but I don't sound like a Cape Coloured?"

"Um … yes. The unfiltered version of my thoughts went something like that."

"And you were worried I'd be offended by your unfiltered thoughts?"

I nod. "People generally are."

"Well, you can add one more person to the list. It's highly offensive that you think all coloured guys should sound the same."

"Uh—"

"How would you like it if I said all white girls sound the same?"

"That's different," I say before I can stop myself.

"Oh, is that so?" Noah's eyebrows rise.

"Well, yes," I say, hoping I can explain this rationally without causing any more offence. "You get Afrikaans white people and English white people and white people who are from Europe or America or Australia or—"

"But coloured people are all the same. You're right. That's not offensive at all."

I cross my arms. "You know, sarcasm really doesn't help."

"Who says I'm being sarcastic? Maybe I'm agreeing with you. Perhaps I see the logic in what you're saying."

I hesitate, trying to figure out from his expression if he's telling the truth. All I can see in his dark eyes, though, is a challenge. I shake my head. "Liar. You don't agree with anything I've said."

"Oh, so I'm a liar now, am I?" Noah slides away from me on the chair. "Next thing I'll be a gangster and a thug too."

I shrug. "Your words, not mine." *Shut up, Andi! Will Damien really appreciate you making his friends angry?* "I'm sorry." I lower my eyes to the scuffed wooden floor. "I didn't mean that."

"Right." Noah stands. "Just like I don't mean it when I say self-righteous, overprivileged white girl."

I breathe in sharply and bite back the urge to tell him he's got thug written all over him. I uncross my arms and stand up. "Well. At least now we know exactly what we think of each other."

I pull open Damien's door and hurry down the stairs before I can do any more damage to the first impression I just made on his friend. I pass a crowd of guys in A quad as I walk briskly along the corridor and wonder if Damien's in the middle of it, dealing with the idiot window jumper. Instead, I find him at reception, talking to someone on the phone.

I sign out and wave goodbye to him, then head outside. Seconds later, I hear hurried footsteps behind me. "Hey, Andi, you're leaving?"

"Yes, sorry, it's getting late." *And your friend and I have exchanged enough rude words for one night.* "Is that guy okay? The one who fell out the window?"

"Yeah, yeah, it's all taken care of."

"Okay, good. Well ..."

"Before you go, I just wanted to check that you're okay

with this," Damien says. "This plan of ours. It's not going to get in the way of our friendship, right? You're happy to do this?"

I give him a smile I hope he doesn't realise is fake. "One hundred percent happy."

WHAT AM I DOING? I CAN'T LIE LIKE THIS. SURE, I'VE NEVER
been one to share deeply personal matters, but I don't *lie* to
people. I simply choose not to tell them things I don't think
they need to know. My friends at school knew I was an only
child raised by a single mother, but I never let them know
she refused to tell me anything about my father. Damien
was aware that I didn't know who my father was, but he
never knew how deeply I longed to discover the truth about
the man my mother wouldn't speak of. And I was okay with
keeping information from those people. That's allowed,
right, as long as I'm not lying?

But now this? This great big deception? Fooling
everyone into thinking we're together? Fooling Damien into
thinking I'm helping him get Marie when I'm actually
hoping he'll fall for me instead? This is *not* me.

My body starts to remember that I'm exhausted from too

little sleep and too much sun, and my steps slow before I'm even halfway across the parking lot. I stop at the rectangular block of stone at the top of the steps leading down to Rugby Road. I climb onto it, tuck my legs beneath me, and stare at the sparkling city lights. I'm lucky enough to have this view from my bedroom window in Fuller. Sometimes I open the window wide and lean out of it, but it isn't the same as being outside and feeling the fresh air all around me.

Don't do this, a quiet voice whispers within me. *Tell him the truth.*

I know my internal voice is right. But I still don't know if there's any point in telling Damien a truth he doesn't want to hear. A truth that will mean the end of our comfortable friendship.

The pretend relationship is still a bad idea, the voice whispers.

I hold my hand over my mouth and yawn a never-ending yawn. I know the voice is right. Faking a relationship isn't the right way to get Damien to notice me. And that's why I'll be telling him to forget about it the next time I see him.

"Wow. This is AMAZING." Livi, the half-sister I found out about last year when I accidentally discovered my real father, steps into my res room with wide eyes and her mouth hanging open. She stands in the middle of the room and stares at all the things I managed to fit in here.

A mound of colourful cushions covers my bed, and since the curtains are so dull, I hung colourful shawls up to cover them. I keep the shawls tied open with ribbons during the day, but now, in the evening, they're drawn closed with fairy lights hanging behind them. More fairy lights are strung across three of the walls, and paper bunting decorates the fourth. The bookcase that was here when I moved in has been filled with my favourite books, and beside it stands a tall plastic storage cabinet, the drawers of which are filled with craft supplies. A second, smaller bookcase houses files—empty at the moment—a kettle, and some mugs and glasses. On the desk stands my laptop, several jars of stationery, a lamp, and a few more piles of books. The last item of furniture is an old armchair, and that, too, is covered by a colourful shawl.

"Did your mom help you do all this?" Livi asks.

"Oh, gosh, no. This isn't her style at all. She's all about the clean, fresh, modern look. This is way more …"

"Cosy."

"Yes." I smile at her. "Exactly."

"And just a little bit magical." She walks to one side of the room and examines the bunting. "Are these triangles cut from the pages of books?"

"Yes. My mom was cleaning out her shelves one day and discovered she had three copies of *Romeo and Juliet*. She threw out two of them, so I rescued them from the bin and made bunting."

"So cool," Livi murmurs, standing on tiptoe to read some of the words. "How did you get all this stuff to Cape

Town?"

"Well, you know, that car I got for Christmas has been pretty useful."

"Oh, of course." She turns to me with a grin. "How's it going with the new car? I mean, the second-hand-but-new-to-you car."

"I love it. How's it going with *your* second-hand-but-new-to-you car?"

"It's amazing." She holds her hand up so I can high-five her. "Thank you, Dad, for the guilt gift."

I scrunch up my nose. "I try not to think of it as a guilt gift and more of an eighteen-years-worth-of-birthdays-and-Christmases gift."

"Yeah, maybe." Livi plops onto the bed. "I think *mine* was more of a guilt gift. He couldn't very well give you a car and not me."

I sit next to her and kick my shoes off. "Well, thanks for coming to visit. It's nice to see you again. Skype is cool, of course, but in person is always better."

"Definitely." She nudges my arm. "So how's it going here? Orientation and friend-making and all that?"

"Pretty good. I like being away from home. I would have gone crazy if I'd stayed there much longer. And friends ... well, I made friends with the girl whose room is opposite mine. Carmen. I'd introduce you, but she's out visiting one of her five hundred family members."

"Right. Big family. Not something I'm familiar with."

I push myself back against the cushions. "Me neither." It was only ever my mom and me, and sometimes a distant relative or two on special occasions.

"Are you aware that you have two different socks on?" Livi asks, tilting her head to the side.

"Yes."

"Okay. And are you still madly in love with The Boy Next Door?"

My skin heats up, and butterflies come to life inside me. Livi's the only one who knows how I feel about Damien. I kept that secret from everyone for so long, but I was starting to feel like I might burst, and as both an outsider and a sister, I figured it was safe to tell Livi. "I am." I drop my head back onto the cushions and sigh. "And now that he lives only a parking lot away, I'm dreaming of him even more."

"You know it's Valentine's Day tomorrow, right?" Livi says, wiggling her eyebrows.

"Yes." I'm very aware of the fact that tomorrow is the night Damien and I are supposed to kick off our fake relationship plan. I haven't seen him since the night I came up with this terrible idea, which means I haven't had a chance to tell him we shouldn't do it. For some reason, I feel like I can't say it in a text message.

"Well," Livi says, forming a heart shape with her thumbs and forefingers and peering through it at me, "perhaps tomorrow's the day your dreams will come true."

Laughing, I push her hands away and sit up. "Okay. Help me decide what to wear for the Valentine's Dance tomorrow night. Maybe if I wear something *amazing*, Damien will finally see me as potential girlfriend material."

HERE'S HOW THE VALENTINE'S DANCE WORKS: THE SMUTS freshmen randomly draw room numbers of Fuller freshmen, and that's the door they show up at just before the dance begins. No one knows beforehand who their 'date' will be. The other girls on my floor have spent all day discussing the possibility of fate sending them their soul mate. I don't blame them. If I wasn't already certain that Damien's the one for me, I'd probably be just as excited as they are.

Since Livi was useless at helping me plan an outfit—all her ideas were far too boring—I spend the afternoon putting my Valentine's Look together. I pick a dress pretty enough to be considered worthy of a not-particularly-formal dance event. It's green with a white paisley pattern, tight at the waist, loose and floaty around my legs, and ends just above my knees. I print out Shakespeare's Sonnet 116, use my flower-shaped punch on it, and stick the resulting flowers to several hair pins. I leave my hair loose, but stick a few pins in here and there. Then, since I have a few flowers left over, I stick one over the front of each of my peep-toe heels. I doubt anyone will notice, but I like knowing my accessories match. Lastly, I dig around in the drawers containing jewellery items I've already made and pull out a long chain with a circular pendant hanging from it. Domed glass covers the pendant, and beneath the glass is a hand drawn heart. Within the heart are the words *i carry your heart(i carry it in my heart)*.

I slip the chain around my neck just as someone knocks on my door. I check myself in the mirror one last time, then cross the room mumbling, "Not a weird guy please, not a weird guy." I pause with my hand on the doorknob, instructing myself to smile no matter who's standing on the other side. I pull the door open, already saying, "Hi!" My face falls at the sight of Noah the Salt Flicker in jeans and a button-up shirt. "Oh. Why are you here?"

"Ah. It's you." He looks about as happy as I feel. "Okay, let's try this again." He closes his eyes, takes a deep breath, then says with a big smile, "Happy Valentine's Day, Andi!" He hands me a paper heart with the words *Be my valentine* written on it.

Hesitantly, I take the heart from him. "Um … I still don't get why you're here."

"The Valentine's Dance?" he says. "The reason you're all dressed up?"

"Yes, I know about that. But I thought it was a fresher thing. First-year students only."

"That's the idea," Noah says, leaning against the door frame. "Doesn't work out so well when there are more girls than guys, though."

"Oh, I see. So you volunteered?"

"Well … roped in is more like it."

"Right. And then you were unlucky enough to pick my room number."

"Yip."

I sigh. "I guess it's going to be a long night. We should probably try to keep our conversation civil and not have a repeat of the last time we met."

"Perhaps. Or we could start over and pretend the other night never happened." Noah gives me a charming smile.

I frown. "So … I'm supposed to forget that you called me a self-righteous, overprivileged white girl?"

"If I can forget that you called me a liar, a gangster, and a thug, then I'm sure you can manage to forget being self-righteous and overprivileged."

I reach for my keys hanging behind my door. "If I remember correctly, you were the one who used the words 'gangster' and 'thug.'"

"You're right," Noah says with a sigh as I pull my door shut. "This is definitely going to be a long night."

Across the landing, Carmen's date is introducing himself to her. I recognise him as one of the guys who offered to help us up a steep part of last weekend's hike. One of the guys Carmen essentially told to get lost. Not a great start. She makes a face at me as Noah and I pass, and I'm not sure if it's because of her date or mine. I roll my eyes to let her know I agree with her either way.

As we descend the stairs, I remind myself to think of Damien and not Noah. Butterflies start doing wacky things to my insides. I'm going to see him in a suit. He'll see me in a pretty dress. Maybe we'll dance together. And then I'll tell him to forget all about our ridiculous plan.

Downstairs in the corridor, older students watch as first years and their dates make their way to the dining hall. Charlotte and her group of followers stand near the doorway, and as Noah and I pass them, Charlotte pretends to look concerned. "Oh my gosh," she says. "I'm so sorry. Did a bird poop in your hair or something?"

I paste a serious look onto my face. "Hmm, I don't think so. Not unless birds poop words."

Noah suppresses a smile as we enter the dining hall. "Friendly girl, that Charlotte. I always liked her. Such a shame she won't be hanging around in Damien's room anymore."

"Yes. Such a shame." We stop just inside the door to look around. I wasn't expecting much after Damien's description, which is probably why I'm pleasantly surprised by what I see. The normally bare rectangular tables are gone, replaced by circular tables covered with table cloths, candles, confetti, and vases of flowers. The dimmed lighting probably also has a lot to do with the improved atmosphere.

"Not bad," Noah says.

"Mmm." I'm hoping if I keep conversation to a minimum, I won't end up saying anything too rude. I check the seating chart and discover we're sitting according to what flat we're in. I look around for familiar faces. "Over there." I point to a table where Kimmy, Georgia and their dates are already sitting.

My butt is barely in my chair when Noah says, "So, what's your story, Andi?"

"My story?" I pull my chair closer to the table.

"Yes. Here's your chance to get the truth out. Prove to me you're not self-righteous and overprivileged."

"I don't think I have to prove anything," I say, angling my body away from him and looking around to see if Damien's here yet.

"In that case," Noah says, leaning back in his chair, "I'll have to continue judging you based on the way you look."

"Fine." I turn back to him. "You want my story? Here it is. I grew up with a single mom and no siblings. I *earned* my spot at the private school I went to, unlike most of the other kids there. Last year I found out I was an accidental consequence of an affair my mom had with a married man. I have a half-sister who's actually pretty cool. My dad's a fancy lawyer dude. My mom's an interior designer who, as it turns out, isn't as good as I always thought she must be because the nice house we've always lived in was mostly funded by Dad's monthly guilt payments. I'm a booktuber, a reluctant university student, and I run an Etsy store where I sell handmade book-related items, because despite the fact that I somehow *look* overprivileged, the only money I have is the money I make for myself."

I take a deep breath, startled at how much personal information I managed to share in one go. What the heck is wrong with me?

"Okay." Noah scratches his chin. "Three comments. One, I guess you're not overprivileged. Two, there's still a hint of self-righteousness about you. And three, I have no idea what a booktuber and an Etsy are."

I stare at him, my mouth hanging open slightly. "How is there a hint of *self-righteousness* about me? You're probably saying that just to get me worked up."

He smiles. "If I am, it's working well."

I snap my mouth shut and clasp my hands together in my lap. *Okay. Be polite, Andi. He wants you to react, so the surest way to annoy him is by remaining calm.* "Booktubers are people who do videos about books," I say. "So, basically, I video myself reviewing books, recommending books, showing off new books I receive. That kind of thing. Then I post the videos on YouTube so other people can watch them."

"And … people find that kind of thing interesting?"

Don't react, don't react. "Other book lovers do, yes."

"Really?"

"Well, eight hundred plus people have been interested enough to subscribe to my channel."

"Eight *hundred?*" The sceptical look on Noah's face vanishes, and he almost looks impressed.

I nod and pick up the spoon in front of me, turning it over and over so my hands have something to do. "That's nothing, though. Some of the really popular book tubers have *thousands* of subscribers."

"And this is all because people want to talk about books and watch other people talking about books?"

"Yes." I tap the spoon against the table. "My friends at school never quite understood my intense love for the written word, which is why I took to YouTube to find like-minded book enthusiasts."

Noah leans back and surveys me. "I think I understand now why you have bits of paper with words on them stuck in your hair."

"Yes." I pat my hair. "I'm pleased you can tell the difference between paper and bird poop."

Noah laughs. It's a pleasant sound. I'm starting to think perhaps we can get past our initial dislike of one another. "And Etsy?" he asks. "What's that?"

"Etsy is a site where people can sell handmade items. Every seller has a virtual store with a store name and all their different products listed. Everything I make and sell has something to do with books. Pin badges with book quotes, necklaces and bracelets with mini books hanging from them, scarves with excerpts printed on the fabric. Stuff like that."

Noah nods. "Okay. I have to admit, that's rather impressive."

"Well, you know, not really." I start turning the spoon over and over again. "I'm certainly not the first to do it."

"Hey, I'm trying to pay you a compliment here," Noah says. "This is where you say 'thank you.'"

"Right, sorry." I give him a small smile. "Thank you."

"You're welcome. So is the Etsy thing working out well for you?"

"Yes, pretty well. I've been doing it almost three years

now. My mom helped me set it up, since I was under eighteen when I started it, but now I manage it myself. Which brings me to the part about being a reluctant student," I say with a sigh. "I want to make crafts and clothes and accessories and talk about books for the rest of my life, but my mother thinks I need a degree, and my dad, whom I've only met once, seems to agree with her. Apparently I'm not being *ambitious* enough."

"And you're a good girl who always does what your mother says?" Noah teases.

I glare at him, refusing to answer that one. "Before we start flinging insults again, how about you tell me your story?"

"My story," he says, then flashes a charming smile at Carmen as she and her date join the table. Carmen stares daggers at him. "My story is this: Born in Durban. Lived in America till I was three because my dad got a contract there. Moved back to Durban for seven years, during which time my sister was born. Then moved to Cape Town. After a few years, my grandmother moved in with us. Then my uncle died, so my aunt and her three kids moved in as well. So that made nine of us under one roof."

"Wow. So … pretty much the same as my experience," I joke.

"Yes, pretty much. I don't think I need to tell you that when a bursary opportunity came up at the end of high school, I was more than ready to leave home and move into res."

"Sounds a bit like Carmen's family," I say, swivelling in

my chair and raising my voice to include Carmen and her date. "She spent the past five years at boarding school, and every holiday her three younger siblings would drive her crazy. She was *very* happy when she discovered her bursary also covered res fees and she wouldn't have to stay at home this year."

Carmen shakes her head. *"Ek's jammer, maar ek praat nie verder met daai ou totdat hy onverskoning vra dat hy my met goed in my gesig gegooi het nie."*

Noah bows his head forwards until it's touching the table. "I sincerely apologise."

After that, it seems a little easier for everyone to get along. Wine bottles are passed around the table, skipping my glass, since I'm of the opinion that wine is gross, and Noah's, because, contrary to what I would have guessed, he doesn't drink. Food arrives soon after the wine starts flowing. I spot Damien at a table for sub-wardens, but he's too busy talking to the people around him to notice me when I try to catch his eye.

When we've finished our dessert and couples begin moving towards the open space of floor intended for dancing, Noah leans over and says, "Do you want to dance?"

I wait for him to start laughing, but it seems he's being serious. Perhaps he thinks he has to offer as part of this Valentine date thing. "Oh, no, we don't have to do that. I'd hate for you to be 'roped in' to anything else this evening." And the only person I really want to dance with is Damien.

"Hey, maybe I like dancing," Noah says. "Besides, one

day you'll look back with great regret that you turned down this opportunity to dance with me."

"Oh really?"

"Yes."

"I'm pretty sure I won't."

"Well, I guess you'll just have to—"

"Hey, Andi. Would you like to dance?" Butterflies assault my insides as I look up and see Damien standing beside my chair. He reaches down and places a paper heart on the table in front of me. It's the same kind of paper heart Noah gave me—I think all Smutsmen attending this dance were instructed to give one to their date—but the difference is that this one has Damien's handwriting on it. And it says *For my valentine.*

I look up again and find Damien waiting with his hand held out towards me. His smile is wide, candlelight sparkles in his eyes, and that suit looks so darn good on him. There is *nothing* that could get me to say no to his invitation.

I push my chair back and stand. "I'd love to."

A THRILL RUNS THROUGH ME AS I TAKE DAMIEN'S HAND. We've never held hands before. Why would we? Friends don't do that. He leads me to the dance floor, and I slide my arms around his neck. My hands are shaking. I hope he doesn't notice. His arms slip around my waist, and we begin moving to the slow beat of the music. He's so close and he smells so good and his eyes are boring into mine and I'm so giddy I might fall over. I have to remind myself to breathe. I have to remind my heart not to leap right out of my chest.

"You're very good at this," Damien says with a conspiratorial smile. "You're almost fooling me."

My pounding heart slows to a painful thud. I look down, breathing in deeply, reminding myself that none of this is real. One dance. I'll let myself pretend for one dance, and then I'll tell him we shouldn't do this.

"You're looking lovely tonight, by the way. Isn't this the

dress you wore when you finally got to meet your dad last year? Just before Christmas?"

I nod and smile, but I can't bring myself to speak. Why does he have to remember details like that? Why does he have to make me feel so important to him when all I am is a friend? Why can't he see that he's perfect for me? That we're perfect for each other?

"I thought so," he says with a smile. "I remember it from the photo you sent me."

I rest my cheek against his shoulder, so that just once, I'll know what it feels like. *One dance*, I remind myself. *Just one dance*.

With a quiet chuckle into my ear, Damien says, "You'll have to keep reminding me that you're not the one I'm supposed to be falling for."

And in that instant, I change my mind.

The Official Mission:

Get Marie to fall for Damien and Mike to fall for Andi.

Step One: Remain friends for a short while.

Step Two: Start fake dating.

Step Three: Take every opportunity to be a happy couple in front of Marie and/or Mike, thereby making them jealous.

Step Four: Bonding as friends—Damien hangs out with Marie and Andi hangs out with Mike.

Step Five: Damien and Andi realise they were only ever meant to be friends and end their fake relationship.

Step Six: Damien gets Marie, Andi gets Mike, and everyone lives happily ever after.

Andi's Side Mission:

Get Damien to fall for Andi instead of Marie.

Step One: Remain friends for a short while.

Step Two: Start fake dating.

Step Three: Damien realises Andi is the one for him.

Step Four: Damien and Andi live happily ever after.

The week after the Valentine's Dance, university starts for real, and I'm plunged into lectures and tutorials and society meetings and a coffee evening with my Fuller mentor and a res charity thing and a few minutes snatched here and there with Damien. After two weeks of trying to keep up with everything, I reach Friday evening, wave off Carmen's suggestion to go out with Kimmy and Georgia, and fall into bed. I only manage to read two pages of my current book before the words start to run into each other, and as much as I'm dying to know what happens, sleep pulls me under.

I surface on Saturday morning to the sound of banging on my door. "Mmm, come in," I mumble, hoping I left the latch unlocked last night. I don't feel like getting up to open it.

"How are you *still* sleeping if you went to bed, like, twelve hours ago?" Carmen asks.

I sit up and squint at her through one half-open eyelid. "I need lots of sleep?"

She walks in and, after moving at least five cushions onto the floor, finds a spot to sit on the end of my bed. "So, I heard a rumour last night that may or may not be news."

"Oh yeah?" I rub my eyes.

"You and Damien—the guy Charlotte broke up with because she thought he was cheating on her—are a couple."

"Oh. Yes. That's news." I give her a big smile.

"Since when?"

"Uh, yesterday." I think it was yesterday that Damien was going to start telling people. I probably should have told someone too.

Carmen purses her lips, then says, "So this is the guy you *weren't* secretly dating?"

"Yes."

"The one you assured me you were just friends with?"

"Yes."

"But now you're together?"

"Yes." I run a hand through my tangled hair. "I've actually always liked him. I've wanted to be more than friends for a while. I guess since Charlotte accused us of being together, he started thinking of me differently."

"I see. And is there a reason you didn't tell me *any* of this?"

"Um ..."

Carmen crosses her arms tightly over her chest. "I don't get you, Andi. You're friendly and self-confident and chatty, but when it comes to anything personal, you close up. You don't share a thing."

"It's not that I—"

"Friends are supposed to tell each other what's going on in their lives, Andi, and I thought you and I were friends."

"We are friends."

"So then?" She gives me a questioning look. "Why don't I know anything about the guy you've always liked or the sister you sometimes visit or why you never answer phone calls from your mom?"

"Because … I mean …" I wish I were more awake for this conversation. "You and I are still getting to know each other. Our friendship is new. There are lots of things I haven't told you yet, but that doesn't mean I'm intentionally hiding them from you. I mean, you haven't told me everything there is to know about you yet, right?"

"Right," she says slowly, but she's still giving me an odd look. "It just seems like it would be normal to talk about the things that are happening *now*. Like Damien." She stands up and heads to the door. "I hope it works out for the two of you."

The door closes behind her before I can say anything else. I flop back onto my pillow, wondering how long it'll take her to forgive me. Hopefully not long, because now that Damien and I are officially together—in the eyes of the rest of the world—I'm more than ready to gush about him the way girls normally do. And I won't have to fake a minute of it.

I check my phone—thirty-five minutes left until the dining hall closes—and find a message from Damien.

Damien: It's official. You're my girlfriend ;-)

I close my eyes and groan, wishing, wishing, *wishing* it were the truth.

What are you doing to yourself, Andi? This is going to be torture.

No. This won't be torture. Not for long, anyway, because pretty soon Damien will forget about Marie and see that I've always been the perfect girl for him.

I shower quickly, then hurry to the dining hall before it closes. After waiting in line for a plate of scrambled eggs, I add a slice of bread to the conveyor toaster. I peer inside the machine to watch the bread make its slow journey along the metal conveyor belt—just as an arm wraps around me.

"Whoa!" I flinch, then relax when I realise it's Damien.

"Hey, gorgeous." He gives me a one-armed hug and kisses my neck—KISSES MY NECK!—before whispering, "I saw Marie heading this way for breakfast, so I figured it would be a good time to start acting like the most in-love couple in the world in front of her. Then you can say you have to rush off somewhere, and I'll stay and chat to her for a bit."

"O-okay. Sounds good." My toast slides out the bottom of the machine. I add it to my plate and follow Damien to the table next to the one Marie and her friend are at. We sit down, and Damien places his hand on my knee. HOW IS THIS SO EASY FOR HIM? My fingers start trembling at the thought of being so close to him, but he's touching my bare skin and chatting away as easily as if we've been doing this for years. Probably because it means nothing to him.

Probably because his attention isn't here, but rather focused on the table next to ours.

I glance up to see if Marie's watching us. She isn't, but a whole lot of other people are. The three girls at the table in the far corner are frowning as they look our way, their lips moving in words I can't decipher. Another two girls whisper as they pass our table, looking back over their shoulders as they head for the door. A large gathering of second-year girls and guys laugh as one of their number stands up, peers our way, then sits back down abruptly. I wonder what they're saying about us.

It doesn't matter.

No, it doesn't. It's never bothered me what other people think. It's just unpleasant knowing that so many of them are probably thinking things that aren't true. But I wanted this, so it's about time I start to enjoy it. I push away the thought of everyone else and lean into Damien, giggling as if I'm about to share a delightful secret with him. "If only Mike were here too," I say. "We could make them both jealous at the same time." And if only I were actually interested in Mike. Then I wouldn't be bothered about the fact that Damien's thinking about another girl when he's with me.

He pulls me closer and kisses my forehead. "Don't worry, we'll have plenty of opportunities."

I allow a dreamy sigh to escape me as I look up into his eyes. No doubt he thinks I'm putting on an excellent performance and that my dreamy sigh and adoring gaze are all an act. I wonder how he'd react if he knew the truth.

By the time I've finished my breakfast, Marie has

definitely noticed us. She's deep in discussion with her friend, but every minute or so, her eyes flick towards us. I'm not excited about leaving Damien here to have a cosy chat with her, but that's the point of our plan, isn't it? Well, the point of *his* plan.

I hug Damien, then rush out of the dining hall towards my urgent, fictional engagement. Once out in the corridor, I slow down.

"I guess the rumours were true."

I look around and see Charlotte coming down the stairs from the upper common room. I start fidgeting with the belt looped through my denim shorts. The belt made from fabric on which tiny words are printed—an excerpt from *Pride and Prejudice*. "If you're referring to the cheating rumours," I say, "no, they were not true. But if you'd like to blame someone for the fact that Damien and I are now together, you can look in the mirror. The only reason we started thinking about taking our friendship to the next level is because you put the idea out there. So thank you."

I spin around and walk away, shocked at how easily the lie came out of my mouth. I hurry up the stairs inside F flat, reaching my landing in time to see Kimmy and Georgia coming out of their rooms. With their slip-slops, hats, and bags bulging with towels, it's clear they're off to the beach.

"Oh, hey," I say to them. "How was last night?"

They exchange an uncertain glance before Kimmy says, "It was fun."

I nod slowly, wondering if they're going to explain the odd looks they're giving me. When they don't, I turn and unlock my door.

"Hey, Andi," Georgia says. I look back at her. "Are you sure … um, is it a good idea to be dating someone who cheated on his girlfriend in order to be with you? Doesn't that mean that he might end up doing the same thing to you?"

"Georgia," Kimmy hisses beneath her breath.

"What? I'm just worried about her—"

"Thanks, but you don't need to be worried," I tell them. "Damien did not cheat on Charlotte."

They look at me, then at one another, then at the floor.

"What?" I demand, just as Carmen's door opens and she comes out. "Carmen, can you please tell them that Damien and I weren't involved in any secret relationship while he was with Charlotte?"

Instead of backing me up, Carmen looks away. She quickly pulls her door shut and heads down the stairs. Kimmy and Georgia follow close behind her. It's only as their footsteps disappear outside that I realise Carmen had a beach towel wrapped around her neck.

I slump against my door frame, confusion and hurt stabbing at my insides. Seriously? Why won't anyone believe me?

Someone jogs up the stairs. I look over the railing and see Damien. The tension inside me eases, and my frown melts into a smile. I didn't realise I'd be seeing him again so soon. "Hey," I say as he climbs the last few steps. "Did you have a good chat with Marie?"

"Yes. Her friend even left us alone for a minute or so. She asked me about cheating on Charlotte, so I told her that wasn't true, of course, along with the rest of our story."

"And she believed you? Because nobody seems to believe me."

Damien steps closer. "What do you mean? What happened?"

I run a hand through my hair and sigh. "Nothing, really. Just that anyone I talk to thinks the cheating story is true, and the people I don't talk to give me weird looks from a distance." I head into my room and make my bed, pulling the duvet straight and putting the many cushions back in place.

"I'm sorry, Andi," Damien says from the doorway. "I didn't think it would be such a big deal. Maybe … maybe we shouldn't do this? I mean, if it's going to alienate you from all your friends, then—"

"No, don't worry about it. My friends will get over it. They'll remember soon enough not to take rumours seriously. And until then—" I cast a glance over the craft supplies on my desk and the piles of lecture notes already building up "—I'll keep myself distracted."

"That's actually what I came up here to talk to you about. My mom just sent a message to ask if I'm going home to visit them this weekend. I was wondering if … you might want to come with? Just for today and tomorrow? I know they'd love to see you."

A weekend with Damien? Just the two of us, away from

the rumours and the stares? YES PLEASE. "That sounds great!" *Jeepers, Andi. Wanna tone it down a bit?* "Uh, when do you want to leave?"

"Well, whenever you're ready."

"Cool." I work hard to keep the rays of happiness from bursting through my smile and blinding him. "Just let me pack an overnight bag."

SIMON'S TOWN IS A BEAUTIFUL SEASIDE TOWN SITUATED ON the shores of False Bay. Houses are built against the side of the mountain rising steeply from the beach, which I imagine gives them a magnificent view of the ocean. Damien turns into the driveway of his parents' house and parks in front of the garage. I climb out and look up. It's a double-storey house with a wide balcony across the front of the upper level. Damien's mom is standing on the balcony waving down to us.

"Do your parents know anything about our pretend relationship?" I ask Damien as I wave back to his mom.

"Hello!" she shouts, then disappears into the house.

"No," Damien says. "To them we're still just friends, so you can relax while you're here." He carries both our bags up the steps, opens the front door, and steps aside to let me in. I have about two seconds to look around—open-plan living and kitchen area with modern furniture, exotic ornaments from their overseas travels, and no clutter—before Damien's mom rushes to throw her arms around me.

"Andi! What a lovely surprise!"

"Hi, Laura." I squeeze her as tightly as she's squeezing me, and it almost feels like I'm back at home, visiting Damien next door.

Next I get a hug from Damien's dad, Ben. *Uncle* Ben, as I used to try and call him. He and Laura insisted on first names only, though, so I gave up on saying 'aunt' and 'uncle' soon after I met them. "Great to have you in Cape Town, Andi," Ben says. "How are you finding it so far?"

"I love it. I'm really happy to be here."

"Wonderful," Laura says. "Well, you can go on upstairs and put your bag down. I'm afraid we only have two bedrooms, so Damien will have to sleep on the couch, and you can have the second bedroom upstairs."

I give Damien an apologetic look, but he shrugs and says, "I think I can handle the couch."

I hurry upstairs, leave my bag in the bedroom that obviously serves as Damien's when he's here on weekends, and run back down for lunch.

"I should probably warn you," Damien says, catching me at the bottom of the stairs, "that my parents are now vegan."

"Oh. Okay. So no meat then."

"Aaand no milk, no eggs, no butter, no cheese. Plus some other things you'd never think would be on the vegan blacklist."

"Right." I twist a strand of hair around my finger as we head for the open doorway leading out to the balcony. "That doesn't leave much, does it?"

"Fruit and veg. That's pretty much it."

"Are you complaining about our food again?" Laura says. She and Ben are already sitting at the table on the balcony. "I thought you enjoyed that spicy red lentil soup I made last time you were home."

"Well, you know, it wasn't a *steak*," Damien says, "but it wasn't bad for a veggie soup."

I sit down beside Damien and survey the platter of food in the middle of the table. Sliced carrot, tomato, spinach and avocado, roasted chickpeas and sweet potato, bread full of seeds, a bean salad, and little bowls of hummus.

"This looks amazing." I nudge Damien's arm. "Who needs steak when you've got a spread like this?"

Damien and I spend the rest of the afternoon wandering through Simon's Town and along the boardwalk beside Boulders Beach. We make a competition out of who can spot the most penguins hiding amidst the beachside bushes—I win—while filling each other in on the details of our lives over the past two years. We've been in contact since he left for UCT, of course—texts, emails, Facebook, the occasional phone call—but many of the small details were left out. Like the fact that the new owners of the house next door painted the outside walls a hideous shade of purple-grey, and that Mrs Donelly, our school librarian, changed her perfume to something that made everyone want to cough.

If life could be like this all the time—just the two of us hanging out and enjoying each other's company—perhaps I wouldn't mind so much that he's never been interested in anything more. Perhaps friendship could be enough for me.

After finding out what Laura's planned for dinner— vegetable curry—Damien tells his mom we'll pick up our own dinner and bring it home. We stop at The Salty Sea Dog, order fish and chips, and drive back to the house. We sit out on the balcony again, talking, laughing, eating, and watching the sky grow darker.

It's late by the time we all go to bed, but I'm happier than I've been in ages. I curl up beneath the duvet that smells mostly of washing liquid but also faintly of Damien's cologne and pray that my future holds many more of these weekends.

Pale morning light filtering through thin curtains wakes me early on Sunday morning. That's another reason I hung shawls across the window in my Fuller bedroom—they help to keep the light out when I want to sleep in. The house is quiet, so I lie in bed listening to the seagulls, checking the

Etsy orders I've received since Friday, and reading the comments on my latest YouTube video.

Emmy Mills (3 hours ago)
This on my TBR list so thanks gonna read it soons.

Apple Turtle (11 hours ago)
OMG I'm reading this book RIGHT NOW! On page 87 and it rocks.

Athena O (17 hours ago)
Thank you for the review and your are so PRETTY!!

One thing about YouTubers? Many of them have atrocious spelling and grammar skills. I often find myself laughing as I read their comments. And then I remind myself that the reason I post videos about books is to connect with people who love reading as much as I do—so who cares how bad their spelling is?

I reply to the comments—even the 'your are so PRETTY' one, which creeps me out a tiny bit—then put my phone down and climb out of bed. I heard someone go downstairs a few minutes ago, which means it's safe for me to emerge. I pull a robe on over my pyjamas and open the door.

"Morning," Damien says as I reach the bottom of the stairs. He's sitting on the edge of the couch, having clearly just woken up. I'm not the swooning type, but seeing him half-asleep, shirtless, and with his normally neat hair all messed up, my insides start to feel a little jelly-like.

I croak out a "Good morning" as he reaches into his bag for a T-shirt and pulls it on.

"Andi, would you like some coffee?" Laura asks from the other side of the counter that separates the lounge from the kitchen. "I remember you being a big fan of our coffee machine."

"That would be amazing, thank you," I say, forcing myself to turn away from Damien. "But, um, I didn't think you'd have milk." I cross the room and lean on the counter.

"Oh, we drink almond milk."

"Imagine my surprise," Damien says, appearing beside me, "when I discovered you can milk an almond."

Laura rolls her eyes. "Don't start that nonsense again." Turning to me, she adds, "It's delicious, Andi."

"Cool, I'd love to try some."

"Great. You two can go on outside, and I'll bring you your coffees."

"Oh, I'll just have water," Damien says. He grabs a bottle of still water from the fridge.

"Are you sure I can't help you?" I say to Laura.

"Of course. Off you go." She waves us away, and we walk out the sliding door and onto the balcony. I lean on the railing and look out at the rippling water. Damien stands next to me, and I'm acutely aware of his arm on the railing right beside mine.

"Did you sleep okay on the couch?" I ask, hoping to distract myself.

"Yes, it was fine. Did you sleep okay in my bed?"

Heat tingles in my cheeks, and I look away so he won't see me blush. "Yes. It was also fine." *Go for a* real *distraction this time, Andi.* I breathe in the salty air and watch several yachts bobbing in the bay. "It's so beautiful here. Like another world. If I were you, I'd come here all the time."

"I used to. I visited a lot last year. I'd bring friends—those who were keen to get away from res for a weekend—but I stuck to solo visits after Noah spent a weekend here."

"Oh, why?"

"My parents had just started the vegan thing, and Noah made a number of comments. I know he was joking, but my parents don't get his sense of humour. They found him really rude. Mom told me not to bring my lower class friends home anymore."

I frown. "She called him lower class?"

"Yeah, well, you've met Noah. He and his family aren't exactly—"

"Here you go, Andi, honey." I turn around as Laura walks towards me with a mug of coffee.

"Ah, that smells so good," I say, taking the mug from her and inhaling. "I've always been jealous of your wonderful coffee machine." I take a sip and—Oh. Wait. Hmm, that's definitely different. "Mmm, that's good," I say, since Laura seems to be waiting for a reaction.

"Great. I'll just grab some fruit and cereal, and I think Ben should be down in a minute. Then we can have breakfast."

I take another sip of coffee, hoping it'll taste better than the first, but—Nope. That definitely doesn't taste right. I try again, a bigger gulp this time, telling myself I'll get used to it. After all, I don't want to waste a mug of—

"Ugh, no, I'm gonna throw up," I mutter, turning back to the railing as the vomit reflex threatens to kick into action. Without a word, Damien takes the mug from me and tosses the contents over the side of the balcony. "Whoa, hey, what are you—"

"Now you know why I'm having water," he says, handing the mug back to me with a sly smile.

I smack his arm. "Thanks for the warning."

SUNDAY EVENING FINDS ME CROSS-LEGGED ON DAMIEN'S couch with an array of craft materials spread around me while Damien sits at his desk working hard on an assignment. I got an order last night for twenty 'So many books, so little time' pin badges, and it turned out I only had nine left. So I gathered up the relevant craft materials in a lunch box and crossed the parking lot to Smuts.

Quiet music plays in the background while I cut out laminated circles and stitch bits of felt together. The only other sound is the *tick-tick-tick* of Damien's typing. Everything is perfect—well, it would be more perfect if we were a genuine couple and there was a whole lot of kissing interspersed amongst the typing and stitching, but it's as close to perfect as I can get right now—until a knock interrupts us.

The door opens and Noah walks in. "Hey, look, it's the

girlfriend." With a nod to Damien, he closes the door, strolls over, and drops onto the couch as if he has nothing better to do than sit here and watch me sew.

"Yes," I tell him. "That's me. The girlfriend."

"Well, you've got a tough act to follow. I mean, that Charlotte. She was a real keeper." Damien scrunches up a piece of paper and throws it at his friend. Noah catches it and presses it into a tight wad between his palms. "Anyway, who wants to help me pick out my new tattoo?"

Damien looks up. "Another tattoo?" He laughs and shakes his head. "I bet your girlfriend will *love* that."

Noah throws the wad of paper back at him. "Fortunately, my *girlfriend* doesn't get a say."

"How about we swap?" Damien says. "You come finish off this assignment, and I'll choose your next tattoo."

"Not a chance, man. You'll pick out some girly butterfly or something."

"And you'll fail my assignment."

"Or," Noah says, "I'll do so well there'll be an inquiry into why your marks have improved so drastically."

"Really? You think your engineering knowledge will help you with this accounting assignment?"

"My engineering knowledge will kick your accounting assignment's ass."

Damien rolls his eyes and turns back to his laptop.

"Andi, Andi, Andi," Noah says, turning his attention back to me. "Is this the stuff you sell on your online craft store?"

"Yes. I'm making pin badges."

"Hmm. I thought pin badges were those plastic circles you pin onto your clothes and stuff."

"Well, this is the homemade version of that. See?" I hold up the creation I'm currently working on. "First I stitch the larger felt circle onto the pin part. Then I stitch the smaller felt circle onto the larger felt circle, and then the laminated circle with the words gets stuck on top of that."

"Huh. And people pay money for that?"

A second ball of paper hits Noah's head, and it fills me with giddy warmth to know that Damien's sticking up for me even when half his attention is on his work.

"Dude, what?" Noah says. "I was joking. Andi knows I was joking, don't you, Andi?"

"Like you were joking during the last conversation we had in this room?"

"You know, I actually was joking at the beginning of that conversation. You're the one who decided to take it up a level by launching into racial issues five seconds after we met."

I lower my hands. "I didn't *launch* into anything. I simply commented on your—"

Damien groans as he looks at his phone. "I have to deal with something. I'll be back just now." He stands.

"You're not on duty tonight, are you?" Disappointment tinges my voice.

"No, but I still need to go check something at reception."

"Okay." I return to the two pieces of felt in my hands,

wondering if Noah will leave now or continue to sit here being antagonistic.

He leans one elbow on the back of the couch. "Guess what," he says.

I apply a blob of glue to the back of a laminated circle and stick it to the two felt pieces I've already sewn together. "What?"

"I know your secret."

The finished pin badge slips from my fingers. I pick it up quickly, checking that the circle is still stuck in the right place while instructing myself not to panic. "Of course you do." I look up at him with a strained smile. "You're Damien's best friend, aren't you? Why wouldn't he tell you our secret?"

"No," he says, shaking his head. He leans a little closer. "*Your* secret."

"My—What do you mean?"

He gives me a smug smile. "You know what I mean."

"Ugh, I hate it when people do that. If you want to say something, just say it."

"Really? You hate it when people do that? Then why don't *you* say what you want to say?"

"And what do I want to say?"

"Oh, Damien, I love you," he coos in a high-pitched voice. "Let's get married and have babies and—"

I grab the nearest cushion and throw it at him. It smacks his face, muffling his words, before landing on his lap. Laughing, he picks it up and throws it back.

"You're an ass," I tell him, hugging the cushion to my chest and crossing my arms over it.

"So I'm right," he says with a triumphant smile.

"I didn't say that."

"Ah, so that means—"

"You know, I think I should leave."

"Hey, no, I'm sorry. You don't have to go. I won't say anything else about … that."

I glare at him.

"Seriously. Here. I'll do the sticking." He picks up the tube of glue and waits expectantly for me to continue sewing felt pieces together.

I pick up a dark blue circle and a pale blue circle and choose a pink thread. After a few minutes of silent stitching, Noah says, "Sooooo, why are you wearing one orange sock and one blue sock?"

"Because life is too short to worry about matching socks," I retort.

"I see."

We go back to not talking.

I stitch.

Noah waits.

I ignore a call from my mom.

More silence.

When I can't take it any longer, I clear my throat and ask, "How did you and Damien become friends?"

"Is this the part where we ask random questions to fill the awkward silence until Damien gets back?"

"Partly. But it's also a genuine question, since you're quite different from the friends he had at school."

Noah rolls the tube of glue in his hands. "You mean the respectable, hardworking, Valedictorian-material friends?"

I smile, already knowing the direction this conversation is headed in. "If I say, 'Yes,' you're going to say something like, 'What makes you think that's not me?'"

"Exactly. And I might also add that you shouldn't judge people because of how they look."

"You mean the way you judged me because of how I look?"

"Hmm. Yes." He tilts his head to the side and considers me. "You've still got a bit of that self-righteous look."

"*How?*" I demand, throwing my hands up. "What are you talking about?"

"Andi." He smiles. "I'm just joking."

"Oh, terrific. You get to insult me and then wave it off as a joke. I should try that." I fold my arms over my chest. "Noah, you look like the kind of guy who might steal my car. Oh, wait, sorry. That was a joke."

Noah blinks, then frowns. "You look at me and you see a *criminal?*"

"Oh, COME ON. You can dish it out but you can't take it?"

"I could take it if it actually was a joke," Noah says, standing up. "The difference is, you're not joking."

"How do you know I'm—"

"Because you're angry," he says simply. He opens the

door. "I'll see you around, Andi." The door swings shut behind him.

I deflate against the cushions, trying to convince myself that I have nothing to feel bad about and wondering why I let this guy get to me so easily in the first place.

I BEND OVER, LINE UP THE CUE STICK WITH THE WHITE
ball, slowly pull the cue stick back, and bring it forwards
fast. The white ball flies across the table, misses the striped
ball I was aiming for, hits one of the solid balls, and sinks it.
It's the first ball I've successfully sunk. If only it were mine.

"Thanks, Andi," my opponent says.

"Okay, it's official. I suck at this." I'm at the George, a
room below ground level at Smuts used mainly for relaxing,
watching TV, and playing pool or table tennis. It's a little bit
like an underground pub—at least, what I imagine an
underground pub to look like, since I've never been in one.

I arrived as the first eight-ball game kicked off. Damien
beat Yashen, then Noah beat Damien, and then Damien
decided I should have a turn. I told him I suck, but he
wouldn't take no for an answer. So I looked around for an
opponent who might also be terrible at pool, and my eyes

landed on Mike sitting on a couch in front of the TV watching rugby. Mike, the guy I'm supposed to like.

"Hey, Mike," I called. "Do you play?"

"Oh, not really. I'm kinda useless at pool."

"Perfect," I said. "Me too."

Twenty minutes later, it turns out there's only one useless pool player in this room, and it isn't Mike. "Here." I hold my cue stick out to Damien. "This is your game now. My pool-playing days are over."

"I guess I should kiss my winning streak goodbye then," Mike says with a good-natured grin as Damien steps up to the table.

"Not necessarily," I tell him. "You're actually pretty good."

"Okay, Damien." Mike does a series of exaggerated arm stretches. "Bring it on. Let's do this."

I laugh, and Damien gives me a raised-eyebrow look that most likely means, *This is the guy you like?*

I shrug and smile back at him, intending for my expression to say something like, *The heart wants what the heart wants.*

I take a few steps back and lean against the bar so I can watch them from a comfortable distance. After a minute or so, Noah leaves the group of guys watching rugby and wanders over to my side. I can't think why he'd be interested in my company after our last disastrous conversation. Perhaps he's come over to get back at me for calling him a criminal.

"Well, isn't this awkward?" he whispers to me. "The guy

you're pretending to date and the guy you're pretending to like—facing off over a pool table."

I ignore him. It's better than throwing verbal punches.

"I'm actually here because I thought I should apologise," he says, pushing his hands into his pockets.

"Oh." I certainly wasn't expecting that.

"I was provoking you," he continues, "so I shouldn't have been surprised when you retaliated. I just didn't realise you'd come up with a jab that hit so close to home. It took me by surprise."

I look at him. "Are you telling me you *are* a criminal?"

He laughs. "No. I'm telling you it's not the first time I've been accused of being one."

"Oh. Well, it was the first time someone's accused me of being self-righteous."

"Probably because you're not." He smiles at me. "Andi, I was just messing with you. I'm sorry. Some of Damien's friends are so uptight I can't help having a go at them."

I frown at the floor. "I suppose I'm one of the uptight ones then, since your comments managed to get under my skin."

"Nah, I wouldn't give you the uptight label." He leans back against the bar. "The uptight friends and family give me horrified looks, then whisper about me when they think I can't hear. You look me in the eye and give as good as you get." He gives me a mischievous grin. "It's a lot more fun."

A smile sneaks onto my face. "Fun, huh?"

"Yip. Besides, no uptight person in their right mind would consider wearing the clothes you wear."

I raise my chin as I turn my gaze back to the pool table. "Well. I hope you meant that as a compliment, because that's the way I intend to take it."

"Absolutely. I can't say I've ever seen anyone else wearing combat boots and a ballet skirt, but you're definitely making it work."

"Thanks." I fluff up my multi-layered tulle skirt.

"Just a word of warning, though," Noah says. "When you bend over the pool table, we can see your underwear."

"Hey!" I smack his arm, and he flinches.

"Ow! Watch the healing wound."

"What healing wound?" I ask, suddenly alarmed I may have actually hurt him. He reaches back for the neck of his long-sleeve T-shirt and pulls. "Whoa, hey." I take a step away from him. "I'm not sure stripping is necessary."

"Relax, Andi," he says with an amused smile. "I've got a vest under here." He removes the long-sleeve T-shirt to reveal a tattoo of a bird across his upper right arm and shoulder.

"Oh, wow, that's cool." I lean forward to take a closer look. "Is it really still a healing wound?"

"No. I was messing with you—again. I had it done the day after I mentioned it to you and Damien, so it's had a bit of time to heal already."

"Okay."

I look across at the pool table as Mike groans and says, "Come on, man. Give me a chance before you annihilate me." He's still wearing a smile, though, so I guess he doesn't mind too much that Damien's beating him.

"Do you have a lot of tattoos?" I ask Noah.

"Just the cross, the bird, and the one on my butt." He gives me a mischievous grin.

I narrow my eyes at him. "You do not have a tattoo on your butt."

He laughs but doesn't answer.

"Why did you choose a bird?"

He pulls his T-shirt back on. When his head emerges, he says, "Birds are free."

"And you … want to be free?"

"Yes." He looks at me as though this should be obvious. "Doesn't everyone want to be free?"

"I suppose. What do you want to be free of?" I ask before stopping to consider whether that might be too personal a question.

He leans closer and whispers, "The demons of my past."

I laugh at his attempt to be dramatic and mysterious. "Oh really? You've got demons hiding beneath that goofy exterior?"

"Goofy exterior?" He does a good job of pretending to be hurt. "And here I thought I was rocking the sexy look."

I laugh. "Well, your muscular, sexy look may do it for some girls, but I'm not one of them."

"Ah, you like the scrawny look, do you?"

I laugh harder and shake my head. Damien and Mike look over at us to see what's going on. "Sorry!" I say. "Didn't mean to interrupt."

They return their attention to the game, and Noah lowers his voice. "You really should go for Mike, then. He's got that scrawny, nerdy look."

"Hmm." I consider Mike. He's about the same height as Damien, but slimmer and with darker hair. He wears glasses, but they suit his face, which isn't that bad-looking. "Actually," I say, "it's more of a *cute*, nerdy look. Thanks for pointing that out."

"You're welcome."

"Perhaps I should go over there and support my pretend boyfriend now."

"Or your pretend love interest. He looks like he could do with some moral support."

Smiling and shaking my head, I walk back to the pool table and stand at one end. "How's it going here?"

"I'm the underdog," Mike says with a relaxed shrug, "so not much has changed."

"Well, that'll make it all the more exciting when you win, won't it?" I flash him an almost-flirtatious smile so Damien can see I'm keeping up my part of the game.

"Hey, don't I get any support from my girlfriend?" Damien jokes.

I blow him a kiss and say, "Sorry, babe." *Babe?* Where on earth did that come from? I've never called anyone 'babe' in my life.

Damien leans over the table, aims his cue stick, and shoots. The ball he was aiming for narrowly misses the pocket, rebounds, whacks a group of three balls, and knocks the 8 ball into a pocket.

"Yes!" Mike pumps his fist in the air, then holds his hand up so I can high-five him.

"Woohoo!" I shout, smacking his palm with mine. "Go Team Underdog!"

"Well done," Damien says with a smile that doesn't reach his eyes, "although it isn't quite the same when you win by default, is it?"

I hurry to his side, remembering that A, I'm supposed to be supporting my pretend boyfriend, and B, Damien's never been a fan of losing.

"You should come down here more often so we can practise," Mike says to medish, oblivious to—or choosing to ignore—Damien's hostility.

"Okay," I say, since our Official Mission includes me spending more time with Mike, and if Damien's around, it'll help out the Side Mission too, which is to make him jealous.

"Great," Damien says, although he sounds anything but pleased. He's doing an excellent job of playing the possessive boyfriend. "Let us know when you're free and we'll both come. I can give you guys some tips."

"Awesome. I'd like that." Mike smiles at Damien, but something about it doesn't look right. Is there a challenge in his gaze? Before I can figure it out, Mike turns and heads back to the TV.

Damien lets go of me, checks his phone, and says, "I'll be back in a few minutes." He heads up the stairs and out of sight.

I grab a cue stick and turn to Noah. "Just you and me, then. Want to show me how it's done?"

His lips turn up. "You're just worried I'm gonna see up your skirt if I stay over here."

"I'm not worried about anything actually," I say as he pushes away from the bar and comes towards me. "You don't know this, but I do the bend-over test every time I make a skirt. I'm fairly certain no one in this room has seen my undies and that you, Noah Ferreira, are once again *messing* with me."

He stops in front of me, that smile still on his lips. "I like you, Andi. We got off to a rough start, but I definitely think I like you now."

"Oh." I reach self-consciously for my hair and tuck a strand behind my ear. "Well, I guess you're not that bad either."

He laughs. "But you are terrible at pool. You definitely need some help."

"And that's why you're here," I tell him as I fetch the white ball. I may as well practise with the balls Damien and Mike left on the table. I lean over, place my hand on the table, and balance the end of the cue stick over my thumb. I line up my shot and slide the cue stick back and forth, trying to judge if I've got the angle right.

"Terrible," Noah says. "I've never seen anything so clumsy."

"Well, a little help would be nice."

Noah steps around me and leans over the table to adjust my hand. "Move your fingers this way—that's right—then hold your thumb against your forefinger."

"That feels weird."

"It'll work better for you. Trust me. And you need to keep your other arm steady when you're moving the cue stick. At the moment you're flapping your elbow around like a chicken with a wonky wing."

I roll my eyes. "Thanks. That's helpful."

The next thing I know, he's standing right behind me, his right hand covering mine on the cue stick and his left arm right beside mine on the table. His chest presses against my back, and I forget to breathe.

"In case you haven't realised," he whispers in my ear, sending a shiver along my neck, "you're asking for trouble. If you're not interested in Mike at all, don't lead him on. And if you really like Damien, just tell him." His steady hand moves the cue stick back and forth. "Okay," he says loudly. "You got it now?"

"Uh huh."

His warmth vanishes as he steps away from me. I suck air into my lungs, slide the cue stick back, and shoot. The white ball skids left instead of forwards, whacks the edge of the table, rebounds several more times, and comes to rest having connected with a grand total of zero balls.

And I don't give two hoots because my mind is still stuck in time about five seconds ago with Noah's arms around me and his breath tingling on my neck.

Trouble. I'm definitely asking for trouble.

"Hey, everyone," I say brightly, waving at the camera set up on its tripod beside my desk. "Today I'm talking about Allison Charmer's new novel, *Circle of Willows*." I hold up the book so my camera can see the cover. "As you know, this book had a lot to live up to after Allison's debut series, *The Broken Cities Trilogy*, was spectacularly well received. So is she as good at writing time travel fantasy as she is at writing dystopian? In two words—" I pause for dramatic effect "—HELL YES."

I spend two to three minutes talking about exactly why *Circle of Willows*—the book I missed four lectures in a row for because I made the mistake of starting it early one morning before breakfast and couldn't stop reading until I'd reached the last page—is so incredible. I urge my subscribers to get their hands on a copy as soon as they possibly can, and add that I loved the book so much I'll be giving away a copy to one lucky person who comments on this video within the next three days.

"And one last thing," I say before I stop recording. "If you didn't see my announcement last week, I've begun a new series of videos titled Cape Town Coffee Shops. Those videos will be posted every Thursday, and each will feature a fabulous new coffee shop I've visited. The first one went up last week, so if you want to know more about Olympia Café in Kalk Bay, you should definitely check it out.

"That's all for now. Happy reading!" I wave goodbye, then stop recording. I remove the camera from the tripod and plug it into my computer. I need to get this video posted quickly because I've still got a tutorial to finish for tomorrow, and it's already 9 pm.

After about half an hour of editing, I upload and publish the video. Then I stand and stretch. I unwind my scarf—made from fabric with 'book freak' written all over it; I like to wear at least one of my Etsy products in each video—and remove my jacket to reveal my pyjamas hiding underneath. The YouTube universe didn't need to see those.

As I settle back into my desk chair and open the relevant textbook, I hear Carmen's loud, contagious laughter out on the landing. I jump up and rush to my door, wondering if today will be the day she stops ignoring me. It's been over two weeks since Damien and I officially 'got together' and Carmen decided I wasn't worth being her friend—or something like that. I keep trying to catch her so we can at least *talk* about this, but she seems skilled at avoiding me. I pull my door open just as she unlocks hers. "Carmen!" I call. She looks over her shoulder, ushers her cousin into her room, and shuts the door behind both of them.

Fine. If she insists on believing Charlotte's rumours rather than listening to the truth from me, then perhaps I shouldn't bother trying to restore our friendship.

I return to my room and slump in my desk chair. I stare at the heart-shaped pinboard on my wall below the *Romeo and Juliet* paper bunting. It's covered in photos, movie tickets, postcards, flyers, brochures, business cards. I removed it from my bedroom wall at home as it was, drove it across the country, stuck it up here, and continued adding to it. Even the Valentine's Day paper hearts from Damien and Noah made it onto the board.

I focus on a photo of me with a group of friends on the last official day of high school before finals began. Those friends are scattered across the country now amongst various universities, and I don't hear from them often. I actually haven't missed them much, but I'm starting to notice my lack of friends here. I need to connect with someone other than the guy I'm in love with and pretending to date.

I swing back around to face my desk and reach for my phone. My hand clenches around the device when I see another two new messages from my mother. I delete them quickly, before the anger has time to take hold, then start typing a message to one of my old friends.

The phone rings in my hand, startling me. I don't recognise the number, but after several rings, I decide to answer. "Hello?"

"Hi, is that Andi?"

"Um, yes."

"Hi, Andi, it's Mike."

"Oh. Hi." I never gave him my number, but I suppose there are several people he could have got it from.

"So, I was just wondering if you want to play pool tomorrow afternoon."

"Oh." I'd actually forgotten about Mike's suggestion that we practise together. It's been more than a week since that evening in the George. "I'm sorry, I can't. Damien's taking me to Truth tomorrow afternoon. You know, the coffee shop?"

"I've heard of it. Uh, what about Saturday morning?" he asks. "Unless you're the kind of person who sleeps in till lunch time. I usually get up early to exercise, and then I forget that a lot of people aren't even conscious until halfway through the day."

I chuckle. "Don't worry, I'm not one of those people. But I've actually got plans on Saturday morning as well. I'm seeing my sister."

"Oh, okay."

I bite my lip and squeeze my eyes shut. This is the point at which I should suggest next week, or next weekend, because he's just being friendly, isn't he? And I could do with more friends. But perhaps he's looking for more, and in that case, I don't want to lead the poor guy on. "Um …"

"Hey, don't worry about it," he says. "We can make a plan another time."

"Are you sure?"

"Yeah, of course. I'll catch up with you in the dining hall some time."

"Okay, great." *You see, Noah? I'm successfully avoiding trouble.*

"And enjoy Truth tomorrow. I've heard their coffee is awesome."

AFTER FINISHING LECTURES AND HANDING IN MY tutorial, I hurry back to Fuller and exchange my varsity bag for a tote bag with 'Reading is sexy' on the side. Normally I'd spend a Wednesday afternoon starting a new tutorial that I'd then have to hand in the following week, but with the lecturer and some of the tutors away on a field trip, I've got the afternoon off. And since Damien has every Wednesday afternoon free, we decided today was a good day to visit Truth.

I sit outside on top of mem stone where Damien agreed to meet me. Instead of facing the city, today I'm facing the opposite direction, admiring the mountain rising steeply behind Jammie Hall. It's impressive. After staring for a while, I pull my phone out and check the comments on my video from last night.

Mallory Hayle (1 hour ago)
Honestly, I preferred her first series, but I'm a major fan
of dystopian books, so that could be why. This one was
also really good.

Shania Martinez (3 hours ago)
So excited 2 read this! Ordered it few days ago and can't
wait 4 it 2 get here!

Prabhati Desai (4 hours ago)
Want to win the book.

LollyMBooks (4 hours ago)
Please pick me, please pick me!!!

Davey (14 hours ago)
Do you love every book you read? Your always giving
five stars to everything.

First of all, I reply in my head, *it's 'you're' not 'your.' And
secondly, I don't give five stars to every book I read, which you'd know
if you've watched every book review video I've posted.*

"Seriously, Andi?"

I lower my phone to find out who's asking me if I'm
serious. It's Charlotte, her perfect curls in a bunch on top of
her head and one hand placed on her hip. I'm sure she's
about to elaborate on the 'seriously,' so I don't bother
asking her to explain.

"What are you wearing?" she asks, her lip curling up in
disdain.

I look down at my tank top, denim jacket, shorts, pink tights, and the sneakers I drew swirls on with a glitter pen when I was bored one day. The pin badge I've got on today is rectangular and says *Keep Calm and Read a Book*. It's pink to match my tights. I raise my head and meet Charlotte's gaze with what I hope is a politely confused expression. "Where I come from, we call them clothes."

She rolls her eyes before marching past me towards Fuller. I return to the comments on my phone, occasionally looking up to see if Damien's on his way over. When there are no more comments to go through, I slide my phone back into my bag and look around. On the Fuller side of the parking lot, a girl executes a painfully slow parallel parking manoeuvre in order to get into her parking bay, and on the Smuts side, Noah walks out and heads towards me. I raise my hand and wave to him.

"Hey, Andi," he says as he reaches me. "So, apparently I look like a messenger, because Damien asked me to come over and tell you something."

"Oh."

"He was on his way out to meet you when Marie stopped by to ask if he could help her with whatever it is they're currently doing in that course they have together. So he's not gonna make it." He pushes his hands into his pockets as my heart sinks down to my glitter-covered shoes. "He said you'd understand, though," Noah adds, "since, you know—" he leans closer and lowers his voice "—it's all part of the plan."

I nod. "Yes, of course, I get it." Still sucks, though. I

hope I'm not about to lose the battle for Damien's heart. I look out over the city, chewing my lip. "Um, maybe I should still go. I need to get a video for tomorrow."

Noah raises an eyebrow. "Video?"

"YouTube thing." I slide off mem stone and pull my bag onto my shoulder. "I'm adding coffee shop videos to my booktubing stuff."

"Cool. Well if you want some company, I'll go with you."

"Oh. Are you sure?"

"Yeah, why not," Noah says with a shrug. "Have you got a car, though? Because unless you want to wrap your legs around a motorbike, you probably—"

"No," I say quickly. "No motorbike. They, um … they scare me." Wrapping my arms around Noah scares me too. I don't need a repeat of that weird feeling that came over me when he got too close over the pool table. "I've got a car," I add. "It's this way."

"This place is so cool!" I stand in the middle of the Truth coffee shop on Buitenkant Street and do a slow three-sixty with my phone camera. "I am seriously digging the steampunk vibe in here." An enormous vintage coffee bean roaster fills the space behind a bar covered in decorative pressed tin panels. The remainder of the café area is filled with leather chairs and copper-topped tables, exposed pipes and oversized cogs, old books and vintage typewriters. The steampunk concept continues into the restrooms with copper pipes, Victorian tap levers, brass basins, and brass extendable mirrors, and even the waiters and waitresses are wearing steampunk accessories.

"I need to get myself a steampunk outfit," I tell Noah as we sit on swing arm stools at one end of the longest table I've ever seen. "That's one thing my wardrobe is lacking."

"Well, if anyone can pull it off," Noah says as a waitress walks over to us, "you can." We place our coffee order, and as she walks away, Noah adds, "You should come here for breakfast. Best French toast in the world."

"In the world, huh? You've tasted all the French toast out there?"

"No. But if I did, I'm certain I'd find this French toast the best."

"I guess I'll have to come back then." I pick up my phone and turn it over and over. "Hey, remember that evening I called you a criminal and you walked out?"

"Of course. One of my favourite interactions with you."

"Ha ha."

"It was."

"Anyway," I continue, "you never actually answered my question about how you and Damien became friends."

"Oh yes, that's true. It's not a very exciting story, though. Damien and I were neighbours in first year. We met each other the first day we moved into res, ended up doing all the O-Week stuff together, and have been friends since then. As simple as that."

"Cool." I nod, turning my phone over and over. "Damien and I were neighbours in Joburg up until he left for UCT. We've been friends ever since he moved next door to me. Also as simple as that."

Noah laughs. "I think we both know that's not true."

My hand stills. "Excuse me?"

He picks up a sugar sachet and points it at me. "You, Andrea Clark, are lying to me."

"I am not." I cross my arms. "Honesty is way up there on my priority list. I don't lie, okay?"

"Honesty's a priority, huh? Then why not tell Damien how you really feel?" A mischievous glint appears in his eyes. "Why not tell him how you *long* for the two of you to be more than friends?"

"I—" I consider denying everything Noah said, especially that part about *longing*, but didn't I just tell him I don't lie? "I haven't lied to him," I say quietly. "I just haven't told him the truth."

"Because ..."

"There's no point. He's never felt the same way about me. It would only make things awkward between us. Probably ruin our friendship."

"What if he's actually secretly in love with you too?"

"Well, you're his best friend, aren't you? Wouldn't you know if that were true?"

"Right. Good point." He taps the sugar sachet against his chin. "I say you move on. Maybe go for Scrawny Mike instead."

I roll my eyes. "You're bad at this. You should not be

giving advice on boys to anyone."

"What can I say? I make a terrible girl."

"Now there's something we can both agree on." On the table beside my hand, my phone's screen lights up, and a song that used to be one of my favourites starts playing. At the sight of my mother's face on the screen, anger and hurt well up inside me. I end the call and turn the phone onto silent, then slip it back into my bag.

"You don't want to answer that?" Noah says.

I paste a smile onto my face. "Nope. She can wait."

His eyes move down to the phone, then back to my face. He frowns.

"What?" I ask.

"Just wondering when last you spoke to your mom."

I narrow my eyes at him, willing the fiery anger burning below the surface not to blaze out of control. "Why?"

"Well, you ignored a call from her when you and I were in Damien's room, and you're ignoring another call now." He places his elbows on the table and rests his chin on his hands. His eyes, which I thought were brown but are actually hazel, never leave mine. "What was it you called yourself that night at the Valentine's Dance? An accidental consequence of an affair your mother had with a married man?"

I try to distract myself with something—the scar above his left eyebrow, for example—but the flames lick painfully at my insides, reminding me of what my mother did. Reminding me of exactly what I am. I never should have told Noah. Somehow, though, things slip out easily around him. Too easily.

"I mean, if it were me," he continues, "I'd probably have major rage issues. I'd be angry with everyone. My mom, the married guy, the world. No doubt I'd end up taking it out on all the wrong people. You, on the other hand, don't seem to be bothered by it. Unless, of course, you're hiding it really well, and one day you'll simply snap."

My smile is brittle. "I have nothing to hide." That's true, isn't it? I'm not *hiding* anything; I'm just not talking about it.

Noah's gaze slips away from mine. "Don't we all have something to hide? Thoughts that torment us when we're alone. Memories that haunt our dreams."

I watch him closely, trying to figure out if this is another one of those times when he's messing with me. But even if he isn't—even if he's speaking of real thoughts and memories—he's no doubt referring to something too personal to ask about. Personal matters should remain personal, which is why he won't be getting the full story about my mother.

"Look," I say, rolling my shoulders to try to relieve some of the tension building inside me, "I won't lie and say that everything's fine. My mother and I aren't exactly getting along at the moment. We haven't spoken much since I found out about the affair and my father, and we haven't spoken at all since I left for Cape Town, but I think that's the way things should be for a while. She should be glad I'm finally out of her way. It's not as though she wanted me in the first place." *Dammit, Andi, just keep your mouth shut.*

"Uh, are you sure you don't want to talk about—"

"Hey, look, our coffees." I give the waitress a wide smile as she places a flat white in front of each of us. Noah's has a leaf pattern on top, while mine looks more like a heart. They both smell amazing. "I'm going to check out the pastry selection," I say to Noah the moment the waitress leaves. "I didn't eat lunch, and I'm quite hungry." *And I don't want to continue our current conversation.*

I take my time examining the croissants, brownies, muffins and cakes, and by the time I've made my selection and returned to the table, Noah seems to have got the message. We don't mention my mom again.

WE'RE DRIVING BACK TO UCT WHEN NOAH LOOKS UP from his phone and says, "Do you mind dropping me off at home? My aunt needs me to fix a TV, and my dad's pretty useless at electronics. Normally I'd tell her to wait until the weekend, but it's my grandmother's TV, and she's kicking up a major fuss."

"Sure, no problem."

"Thanks. It isn't far. Only about ten minutes from UCT."

"*Ten minutes?*" I look over at him, then back at the road. "Your home is *ten minutes* from UCT, but you live on campus?"

"Nine people under one roof, remember? I had to get out."

"Oh yes. That must have made you a little crazy."

"More than a little, I think." He turns the radio up and

smacks out a rhythm against his knees while occasionally pointing out which way I should turn. When we arrive in front of his house, he says, "Thanks so much. Do you want to come in?"

"Oh, no, I should probably get back to Fuller. If I wait here much longer I'll get caught in traffic on the way back to campus. A ten minute drive will end up taking at least half an hour." I don't add that the idea of his large family scares me a little.

"We'll stay for dinner," Noah says. "Leave after the traffic. Trust me, the food here is *way* better than in res. And this way I won't have to call you later to ask you to come back and pick me up," he adds with a grin.

"Oh, of course, you also have to get back to campus. Sorry, I don't know why I didn't think of that. Um, yes, okay. I'll stay." I turn the car off and climb out.

Noah rings the bell. "Didn't bring my keys," he explains.

I nod, rubbing my hands over my shorts. The memory of standing on Damien's parents' balcony on a morning not too long ago pops into my head. *Mom told me not to bring my lower class friends home anymore.* I push the thought away. I don't want to judge Noah's family before I've even met them.

"So, just to warn you," Noah says, "it's probably quite noisy in there. My three cousins are boys. All under the age of twelve. They have a lot of energy to expend. And since Grammy's TV's not working, she'll be adding to the noise."

I continue nodding. "Cool. I can handle noise."

The gate rolls open, and we walk up the driveway as the

front door opens. "Noah, thank the Lord," an older woman says as she leans out. "Grammy's been yelling at her TV for an hour."

"Sounds about right," Noah says, stepping up to the front door and giving the woman a brief hug. He turns back to me. "Andi, Auntie Shaylene. Auntie Shaylene, Andi."

I greet Noah's aunt and follow the two of them inside. A small boy runs past us, shouting, *"Ek kon dit nie daar kry nie."* An answering shout of *"Kyk harder!"* comes from upstairs, just as an older man's voice yells, "Stop shouting!"

Noah glances at me and shrugs. "It's like this a lot."

We head down a passage, past a kitchen and several closed doors, and into a room with an unmade bed, a dressing table covered in old perfume bottles, jewellery, and medication, and an ancient TV in one corner. In front of the TV, sitting in a wheelchair, is a grumpy, grey-haired woman.

"Hey, Grammy," Noah says cheerfully. "How's everything going?"

Instead of answering, Grammy looks past Noah and frowns at me. With slow, slurred words, she says, *"Wie's daai wit meisie?"* Her shaky right hand tugs at Shaylene's sleeve. *"Vir wat is sy hier?"*

Shaylene gives me an apologetic look, then mutters, *"Ma, moenie onbeskof wees nie."*

"Sorry," Noah says quietly to me. "I should have warned you about Grammy. She had a stroke two years ago and lost the use of her left side and, apparently, her filter. She pretty much says whatever comes to mind. So don't be offended."

"Well, I am the palest person I know," I say, raising my

arms in front of me, "so I shouldn't really be offended by the label 'white,' should I?"

Noah grins. "You are very white, aren't you?" He crosses the room to the TV, pulls it away from the wall on its wheeled trolley, and slides behind it. "So, you're having TV troubles again, Grammy?"

"*Dom masjien*," she grumbles, waving the remote control at it.

Shaylene rolls her eyes and walks back to where I'm standing in the doorway. "Come on. You don't have to stay here and listen to the old lady cursing her TV. You can meet everyone else." She takes me around the house and introduces me to Noah's father in his study, Cousin Number One, Number Two, and Number Three who are arguing over TV channels in the lounge, and Noah's mother as she arrives home from work. I remember Noah mentioning a sister, but she doesn't seem to be around.

"All fixed," Noah announces, appearing in the doorway of the kitchen just as I've finished giving Shaylene and Noah's mom the edited version of my life story. "Hey, Ma," he adds. "Is it cool if we stay for dinner?"

"Of course. You've seen the size of the curry pot, right?" She points to the stove where a pot bigger than any I've seen before sits. "You know Shaylene always makes enough to feed an army."

"Ah, but did she make enough to feed *Andi*?" Noah says, throwing me a teasing smile. "This tiny girl over here eats a deceptively large amount. You should have seen the size of the cake she had at Truth."

"Hey, I offered you some of that cake and you weren't interested," I remind him.

"Because it had carrot in it. Vegetables have no business being anywhere near a cake."

"Carrot cake is the best cake in the world," I tell him authoritatively.

"Agreed, Andi," Shaylene says.

"You guys are crazy," Noah says as his phone rings in his pocket. "French toast is the way forward."

"*Nie vir middag tee nie*, silly," Shaylene says, flicking him with a dishtowel as he removes his phone from his pocket. I see a picture of a pretty girl on the screen before he steps out of the room to answer it. Half a minute later he returns, saying, "Lolly said she'll be here in half an hour."

His mom nods as she pulls a bag of rice from the cupboard. "Great."

"Want something to drink, Andi?" Noah pulls the fridge door open and examines the contents. "I can offer you … orange juice or water. That's it."

"Water's great, thanks."

"Sure?"

"Yes. Beats almond milk any day," I add.

Noah leans around the fridge door and gives me a questioning look.

"Damien's parents," I explain.

"Ah, yes. The vegan thing. I don't think they appreciated my comments on their dietary choices." Noah hands me a glass of water, then takes a swig of his orange juice.

"Is Lolly your girlfriend?" I ask.

Noah chokes on his juice. "Girlfriend?" He coughs while his mother and aunt laugh at the two of us. "No, she's my sister."

"Oh." Now I understand the laughter. "Oops. Well, when will I get to meet your girlfriend?"

He gives me a confused look. "I don't have a girlfriend."

Now it's my turn to be confused. "But … when you were talking about getting a new tattoo, Damien very sarcastically said your girlfriend would love that, and you said—"

"Oh, no, no. That's not—No, definitely not." He laughs. "Damien was talking about a girl in one of my classes. We went out once, and then she became a bit of a stalker. Damien likes to refer to her as my girlfriend because he knows it annoys me. She's a bit weird. Still shows up at Smuts sometimes asking for me."

"That's a bit awkward."

"Yip. I've told her repeatedly—in the nicest possible way—that she and I will never be together."

"Maybe you're being too nice."

He runs a hand over his barely-there hair. "Trust me. Nice is the only way to go with this one. The one time I tried to be a little firmer, she completely flipped out. Starting yelling at me about being racist, that I wouldn't date her was because she was white. I think the whole of Upper Campus heard her."

"Oookay."

"Noah, Noah, Noah!" Noah's smallest cousin dashes into the kitchen from outside and tugs at Noah's arm. "Can we do Savage Time? Pleeease?"

"Yes, Noah," Shaylene says, giving him a pointed look. "*Please.*"

"Fine." Noah allows himself to be dragged outside to the garden.

"Savage Time?" I ask. "Do I even want to know?"

"Best thing ever," Shaylene tells me as she removes a whole load of knives and forks from a drawer. "Noah came up with it when Jamie—my youngest—was four. It's for when they've all finished homework and have *way* too much energy for me to deal with. They go outside and Noah chases them around. If he catches them he'll toss them over his shoulder or hang them upside down or ... something. I don't know. I don't generally watch. I think sometimes the three younger ones gang up and attack Noah. Whatever the rules are, it generally ends up with all four of them attacking each other in a heap on the ground. Fantastic way to exhaust the boys."

"Sounds ... fun?"

"I don't suggest you go outside," Noah's mom says. "I got knocked over once when I went to call them for dinner. Now I just shout from the window."

"The window definitely sounds safer. I'll watch from there."

Half an hour later, Savage Time is over, dinner is ready, and ten of us are squished around the dining room table. Noah and the three boys are covered in dirt—except for their hands, which they were forced to wash—Noah's dad is trying to have a conversation with Grammy—who won't stop complaining about the food, and then tells everyone she needs to go to the toilet RIGHT NOW—and Lolly is giving an animated description of her afternoon soccer practice to her mother and aunt. It's nothing like any dinner I've ever had with Damien and his parents, and it's light-years away from the dinners Mom and I used to share every evening. We chatted, of course—at least, we did before I found out about my father—but the chatter of two people can never come close to that of ten.

I love it. I love that there's never a silent moment I feel obligated to fill. I love that I can barely hear the clinking of cutlery amidst the talking, laughing, complaining, squealing, and interrupting. I love that at one point I'm involved in three different conversations at the same time. They speak partly in English and partly in Afrikaans, and I assume the English is for my benefit until Noah mentions that his dad was brought up in an English-speaking home.

On the other end of the table, Lolly laughs loudly, then lowers her voice to a whisper while watching Noah and me. "Um, I get the feeling they're talking about us," I say to Noah.

"I think you're right." He spears a curried potato with his fork. "They're probably taking bets on whether you really are just a friend or if we're actually together."

"Perhaps we should make a general announcement just so everyone knows."

Noah gives me his mock serious face. "Why? Don't you think there's a chance we'll wind up together one day?"

I laugh. "You're not exactly my type."

"And what is your type, Miss Clark?"

"Well, Mr Ferreira, it isn't tattooed and wearing a wife-beater."

With a chuckle and a shake of his head he says, "That's right, I forgot. You don't actually have a type. You have a *person*. A person who's probably never even owned a wife-beater." He shovels more food into his mouth, chews, then adds, "Just out of interest, have you ever liked anyone other than Damien?"

"No, of course not. Damien's always been the one for me."

"Why?"

"Hmm?" I pause to chew on a mouthful of curry and rice.

"Why Damien?"

"Well, he's just … always been there for me. If school was horrible, he was there at the end of the day to make me feel better. When I got lonely and needed someone to hang out with, he was just one house away, and he understood my loneliness because he doesn't have brothers and sisters. If I fought with my mom and wanted to get out, his house was the one I'd run to. And he's always supported my YouTube and Etsy stuff. He even used to help me with some of the crafts."

"Sounds perfect," Noah says.

"Exactly."

"And really boring."

"Hey!"

"Have you guys ever fought about anything?"

"Of course not. Fighting's bad."

"No it isn't. Fighting is honest. Sometimes you've just gotta get everything out there. All the issues and stuff."

"Well, we don't have any issues," I say. "And if we did, we'd just talk about them rationally."

"Everyone has issues. No one's perfect."

"Maybe *you* have issues," I say, pointing my fork at Noah, "and maybe I do too. But Damien? He's pretty close to being perfect. And Damien and me *together*? That's gonna be close to perfect too."

"Well then," Noah says, raising his glass of orange juice. "Bring on the most boring couple of the year."

We get back to campus just before 9 pm. "Thanks again," Noah says as we reach the parking lot between Fuller and Smuts. Hopefully next year I'll be fortunate enough to get a spot up here rather than having to park down the road.

"No problem. It was nice meeting your family. I like them."

Noah's smile seems relieved. "Good. I don't take many friends home. I never know if Grammy and her rudeness will be too much for people. Damien didn't like being called 'that white boy,' so that visit turned out awkward, to say the least. But Grammy told me you're allowed to visit again, so you must have made a good impression."

I look down at my shoes and smile to myself. Now I've heard both stories: Noah's visit to Damien's family, and Damien's visit to Noah's family. Sounds like neither of them went particularly well.

"What are you smiling about?" Noah asks, tilting his head.

"Oh, nothing really." I shrug. "It's just funny you and Damien ended up friends when you come from such different families."

"I guess it is." He rubs the back of his neck. "Anyway, uh … have a good night."

"You too." I step away, but he steps towards me, obviously moving in for a hug. There's an awkward moment of fumbling limbs until we finally end up with our arms around each other, laughing. That moment by the pool table flashes through my mind. Noah's arms around me. His hand over mine on the cue stick. His breath leaving chills along my neck.

I force my mind in a different direction.

We part ways after the hug, and I wander slowly back into Fuller, enjoying the warmer-than-usual evening air. I contemplate calling Damien. I'm torn between wanting to hear his voice and *not* wanting to hear what a great afternoon he had with Marie.

I reach my floor inside F flat and find Carmen pacing across the landing, speaking rushed Afrikaans into her phone, her face wet with tears. She ends the call and hurries back to her room without saying a word to me.

"What's wrong?" I ask before she can close her door.

"None of your concern," she mutters.

"Carmen, come on. Just let me help y—"

"My grandpa had a heart attack, okay?" she snaps,

spinning around in the doorway to face me.

"Oh my goodness." My bag slips to the floor. "Is he …" I can't bring myself to say it. *Dead.* "How is he? Have you seen him?"

"Of course I haven't seen him, Andi," she shouts. "How am I supposed to get to the hospital? I don't have a rich father like you ready to just hand me a car."

Her words sting, but I decide not to go there. "What about—"

"All my family members with cars are already there, and they don't want to leave Grandpa. One of my cousins said he might come get me a bit later, but I don't want to wait that long."

"Well, I'll take you. I don't mind—"

"No. I don't need your help." She steps back and starts shutting her door.

"Carmen, wait." This hating me thing is starting to get old. "Look, I get that you're upset about your grandfather, and you're upset that I didn't tell you what was going on with Damien. But I've apologised for that and it's in the past, so why can't you stop being so mad at me? Why can't we go back to being friends?"

She stares at me, slowly shaking her head. "It's amazing how convincingly you lie."

"*What?*" I hope she can see how baffled I am because I don't think I can put it sufficiently into words.

She speaks slowly, looking at me as if I'm stupid. "Damien cheated on his girlfriend. With you. Then you lied about it. To my face. Twice. Now I'm sorry, but I can't be friends with a compulsive liar."

"I told you that's not—"

She takes another step back and slams her door shut.

I stare at the door, my breath quickening and my insides burning up. Noah was right. On the surface, I don't seem bothered by things that should upset me. Tell me there's poop in my hair, and I'll come up with a civilised response. Insult my clothing, and I'll act politely confused. Spread rumours about me, and I'll shrug them off. Tell me I was an accident and never wanted by either of my parents, and I'll push the hurt down where I don't have to feel it. But underneath it all, I'm a ticking bomb waiting to explode on the unfortunate person who happens to lay the last proverbial straw.

Carmen is that person.

I march across the landing and push her door open with such force it bangs against the wall. "I have had ENOUGH of these ridiculous accusations," I shout at her. "I don't know what you heard that could possibly have convinced you so thoroughly that I'm a compulsive liar, but whatever it was, it's NOT TRUE. I may have kept things from you because, HELLO, we've only known each other a few weeks, but I have NEVER LIED TO YOU. Now stop being so damn STUBBORN and let me bloody well DRIVE YOU TO THE HOSPITAL."

I sit in a hard, plastic chair under bright lights drinking bad coffee and waiting for Carmen. Her extended family has just about taken over the whole waiting area, but I managed to find a seat in the corner next to Carmen's cousin Tania. I pretend to read an ebook on my phone while processing my thoughts.

Friends are supposed to tell each other what's going on in their lives, Andi, and I thought you and I were friends.

I thought we were too, which means I should have told her what was going on with Damien. Why didn't I tell her? Why didn't I realise that something BIG DEAL, like the guy I've loved for what feels like forever, should be shared with her?

My thoughts tumble back and forth as my eyes scan the same paragraph over and over, seeing the words but taking in nothing. Eventually, Carmen walks over and places a hand on Tania's shoulder. "You doing okay?" she asks.

Tania raises her head from her arms, and I notice her red eyes. "I hate hospitals so much," she says. "They always make me think of—" *sniff* "—Tyrone and Ferry."

"I know," Carmen says gently, rubbing Tania's shoulder. "Do you mind if I sit here so I can talk to Andi? Your mom's over there. I think she got you something to eat." Tania wipes her face, sniffs again, and stands. Carmen collapses into the chair, running a hand over her frizzy hair. "Her twin brother was in a car accident a few years ago," she says, watching Tania walk away. "He didn't make it."

"Hectic," I murmur. I have no idea what to say to something like that. I've never dealt with death before.

"Yeah. Anyway, thanks for waiting," Carmen says, rubbing her eyes. "No one lives near campus, so no one really wants to drive me back there. I appreciate you helping me out after … you know. My unreasonable bitchiness."

"Hey, this is big deal stuff. Of course I'm gonna help you out." I lock my phone and return it to my bag. "How's your grandfather doing? Have you seen him?"

"No, but the nurses say he's stable, which I suppose is as good as it gets after a heart attack. I have to come back tomorrow during visiting hours if I want to see him, so that means we can head back now."

"Oh, are you sure? You don't need to stay for anything else?"

She shakes her head and yawns. "My parents are gonna stay a bit longer, and maybe some of my aunts and uncles, but if we're not allowed to see Grandpa, then …" She shrugs. "I guess there's no point in staying. And I feel a bit better now that I've been here and heard everything the nurses and doctors have to say. It's still horrible, and I keep praying he doesn't die even though I *know* he's old and it could be his time to go, but I just … I'm glad I came. Thanks for bringing me."

I nod. We stand up, and I take a slow walk to the elevators while Carmen says goodbye to everyone. Once we're back on the road, silence fills the car like a tangible presence. I've got a lot to say, but I'm waiting until we reach the highway before I launch into everything. "Okay," I say once we're on the highway and I've got no more turns to worry about. "I thought about a lot of stuff while I was sitting in that waiting room, and I realised I haven't been nearly as open with you as I could have been."

"Andi, it's fine, really. Like you said, we haven't known each other long. I shouldn't have expected you to spill everything going on in your life."

"Well, no, not everything, but I should have told you about Damien. I think the problem is that I'm used to keeping things to myself. I had girlfriends at school, of course, but somehow I never confided in them about anything major. Not even when I found out about my mom's affair with a married man—"

"What? Really?"

"Yes. A guy who turned out to be my dad. And I've been head over heels for Damien for *years*, but I didn't tell my friends that either in case it got back to him, which would have totally ruined things between us. And now that those friends are scattered all over the country, the friendships I had with them are just … drifting away. And I think it's because I never shared anything about myself. If any major issues came up, I generally ended up sharing them with Damien and no one else. So I'm starting to think that maybe the picture my friends had of me wasn't the real one. It was happy and problem-free and … fake."

"I'm guessing Damien knows the real you, though."

"Yes," I say with a sigh. "Or maybe not. Maybe he also only sees the things I want him to see, and none of the deep-down, horrible stuff. But while we're on the subject of

Damien …" I take a deep breath and tap the steering wheel with my fingers. It's time to lay it all out there. I can't have a real friendship with Carmen while keeping something like this from her. "There's something you should know about our relationship. It isn't … actually … real." I remove my eyes from the road for a moment to check her response. She's watching me closely, her eyebrows raised. I return my eyes to the road, rushing into the rest of my explanation, filling her in on every detail.

When I get to the end, she says, "Eish, now I kinda wish you were lying to me."

"So … you don't think it's a good idea?"

"It's a terrible idea, Andi! It's like you're *asking* to have your heart broken."

"I know, I know. There's that risk. But if it works out, it'll be worth it. I think he's starting to see me differently already."

"Really? Or are you just trying to convince yourself of that?"

"I … I don't know. Anyway, the more important thing here is whether you believe me or if you still think everything I say is a lie."

I look at her again, and she smiles. "I believe you."

"You do? What convinced you? I mean, you seemed quite certain earlier when you were calling me a compulsive liar."

"Um …" She leans her head back. "I thought I had evidence that you and Damien were together last year, and then you totally flipped your lid earlier, which I've never seen you do, and it made me think about that *evidence* I thought I had, and I realised it was actually nothing to do with you."

"Evidence? What are you talking about?"

She sighs. "It doesn't matter now."

"If it's Charlotte's friends saying they saw me with Damien last year, well, that is true. We were together—as in, sitting next to each other—but we weren't *together*."

Carmen starts playing with the buttons on my radio. "I know."

"But you still don't think we should be doing this fake relationship thing."

"I think …" She sighs, leaves the radio on a channel playing classical music, and leans back. "I really think we should tell people the things we need to tell them before it's too late. Grandpa and my dad have been angry with each other for years because of some disagreement about my mom, and now all my dad can feel is guilt because it might be too late to work things out. My cousin Tania still hates herself because the last thing she and her brother did before his car accident was fight. She alternates between wanting to kill Ferry, the guy her brother was with who survived the accident, and wanting to kill herself."

"Jeepers."

"Yeah. Life sucks sometimes. There are a lot of things we can't control, but we can at least control what we say to people. It's better than leaving it until it's too late."

I nod slowly, my thoughts swirling in every direction, darting past pros, cons, dreams, hopes, regrets, consequences, and finally coming to a single undeniable conclusion.

I have to tell Damien the truth.

CARMEN AND I ONLY GET TO BED AROUND MIDNIGHT, which means I feel like a zombie when my alarm goes off at 6:30 am the next morning. How do people survive on less than eight hours of sleep? I convince myself to sit up, but I can't keep my eyes open, so I stay in that position for a while, slouched over, eyes closed, half conscious.

A door slams on the landing upstairs, startling me from my lethargy. I push myself to the edge of the bed and drop my legs over the side. One step closer to being up. I reach for my phone and turn it over. When I see all the missed calls and text messages, I realise I haven't looked at my phone since Noah and I left Truth yesterday. The first message is from Mom—**I know you don't want to talk, but just let me know you're okay please**—which I reply to quickly before she does something embarrassing like calling the Fuller warden to track me down. The remaining alerts are from Damien. Two texts—one apologising for bailing on me yesterday afternoon, and one asking where I am—and three missed calls.

I touch the call button and bring the phone to my ear. He answers after three rings. "Hello, Andi?"

"Yeah, it's me. I just saw all your calls now. Is something wrong?"

"No, no." He hesitates. "Are you … mad at me?"

"What? No. Why?"

"It's just that you normally reply to messages and return calls pretty quickly. When I didn't hear from you or see you in the dining hall last night, I got worried."

He was worried about me! How sweet. I guess I do reply to his messages far too quickly. I need to practise restraint. "I'm so sorry, I didn't mean to make you worry. I was with Noah."

"Noah?"

"Yes, he came with me to Truth, and then we had dinner at his family's house."

"You … had dinner with his family? I didn't realise you guys were so friendly."

"Um …" I rub my eyes with the heel of my free hand. "I don't know. I guess we are. He had to fix his gran's TV. Then Carmen's grandfather had a heart attack so I drove her to the hospital. We got back late. I guess I was so tired I forgot to check my phone. I'm really sorry."

"No, don't be. I'm glad you're okay. I need to get going, so I'll see you later."

"Okay."

I spend a large portion of my lectures replaying the phone call in my head—in between yawning, which I also do a lot of—and trying to figure out if Damien was upset about something. He said I shouldn't be sorry, but he sounded a bit odd when he said he needed to go. When I'm done contemplating the phone call, I try to convince myself that I'm brave enough to tell Damien how I really feel about him. I start writing down what I should say, but I end up crossing most of it out. Nothing sounds quite right.

I don't see Damien in the dining hall during dinner, so I type a message reiterating how sorry I am for making him worry about me. Then I remember I'm supposed to be restraining myself when it comes to texting Damien so I don't appear too desperate for his attention. Then I wonder if I should simply be typing 'We need to talk' so that next time I see him I'll be forced to tell him the truth. In the end, I delete what I've written and send nothing.

Carmen's staying at home for the next few days so it's easy for her to get to and from the hospital with her family. No Damien *and* no Carmen means I'm eating dinner alone. Not the most pleasant of experiences, even for someone like me who doesn't care too much what other people think. After this happens two nights in a row—with little more than a 'Sorry, I'm REALLY busy' message from Damien—I pack my dinner into a container and head back to my room to eat it there. Before I reach F flat, Charlotte steps out of H flat and stands in front of me.

Oh great. This again. "Don't bother," I say, holding my hand up before she can get a word out. "We both know how this exchange is going to go. You'll tell me that my clothes are weird or that red hair is ugly or that Damien and I are doomed to fail because we're both cheaters. Then I'll inform you that I actually love both my clothes and my hair colour and remind you once again that Damien never cheated on you. So let's just skip to the end, shall we?"

She frowns at me, somehow managing to remain annoyingly pretty while doing so. "What are you talking about? Your hair isn't *red.* Nobody's natural hair colour is actual, real *red.*"

"I see. Well, now that we've cleared that up, I'll be on my way."

"What I *was* going to say," she adds before I can step past her, "is that I noticed you're now keeping company with both cheaters and drunks."

"Oh, is Damien a drunk now as well?"

"Not Damien, you idiot. Noah Ferreira. Don't you know anything?"

"Well I certainly don't know *everything*, but I do know that Noah doesn't drink."

An irritated sound comes from her throat. "You really don't know anything, do you."

"I guess not." I walk around her and continue on my way. No way am I going to ask Charlotte what she's talking about. I won't give her the satisfaction.

I eat dinner while sitting cross-legged on my floor and

examining my pile of unread books, trying to decide which one to pick next. Then, since I've got neither Damien nor Carmen to hang out with, and no assignments, tutorials or Etsy orders to finish, I decide to get a head start on next week's book review video.

I set up my camera beside my desk and pick up *The Italian Hoax* from my book shelf. I finished reading it yesterday morning just before I had to rush to lectures. I'm about to start recording myself and the book when someone knocks on my door. I drop the book onto my chair, cross the room, and open the door.

"Hey, Andi," Noah says.

"Oh, hi. What's up?"

"Just looking for Damien. Thought he might be here."

"No, sorry, I haven't seen him today."

"Oh, okay." His gaze slides over my shoulder. "Sheesh. Do you like cushions, by any chance?"

I turn around and consider my bed. "Yes. Apparently I'm a cushion hoarder."

"Where exactly do you sleep? On the floor?"

"Look, I'll admit it's a challenge at times, but somehow my cushions and I manage to share the same space."

"And what if there was a *person* hoping to share with you?" His cheeky grin surfaces.

"Well, that person would have a problem, because no matter how many cushions I remove, it won't change the fact that residence beds are possibly the narrowest beds in creation. I think they rival prison beds."

"Probably." He looks over my other shoulder. "So. I see

the camera's all set up. Are you getting ready to gush over a book?"

"Yes, which is why you need to leave now."

"Oh come on. Let me stay. I want to watch."

"No. Way."

"Okay, let me be in it then. I bet your subscribers will love me."

"No."

He walks past me into the room without waiting for an invitation. "Is this the book?" he asks, picking up *The Italian Hoax* from my chair. "Cool. Let's do this."

I cross my arms. "You haven't read the book. How are you going to talk about it?"

"Well, you can give a review based on the content, and I'll talk about the cover."

I give in with a sigh and close the door. "Fine. But if it's terrible, I'm reshooting the video when you're not around."

"Fair enough."

I swing the tripod around until the camera faces the bed so Noah and I can both sit down. I reach for the camera's remote control. "Okay, I'll start off and you can … I don't know. Add in your two cents whenever you feel like it."

"Awesome."

I start the recording and place the remote on the bed beside me. "Hey, everyone." I wave at the camera, and after a second's pause, Noah does too. "I'm Andi and this is Noah, and today we're talking about *The Italian Hoax*." I hold the book up for the camera to see.

Noah points to the cover and says, "Check it out, ladies.

There's a hot guy for you. If the story gets boring, you can stare at him instead."

"I can assure you, though," I say quickly, "that you won't be getting bored. After having to wait almost two years, our favourite paranormal investigator Becky is back, and—"

"Woohoo!" Noah's shout startles me. I stare at him with wide eyes. "Sorry," he says. "Inappropriate response?"

"No, entirely appropriate, actually." I turn back to the camera with a smile. "We fell in love with Becky in book one, our hearts broke when we read what happened to her in book two, and now that she's back and just as badass as ever, you'll have to work hard not to cheer out loud when she kicks this villain's ass. Or—" I lean forward and lower my voice slightly "—if you're like me, and you know you simply can't contain yourself, make sure to read this book in private so you don't startle strangers with your sudden exclamations of excitement."

Noah regards me with raised eyebrows. "I wish I'd been around for that."

"No you don't. I might have accidentally hit you when punching the air and shouting 'yeah.'"

Noah considers that. "Sounds like a risk I would have been willing to take."

"Aaand back to the book," I say, looking at the camera once more. "Mystery abounds, a new twist will shock you at every corner, and the romantic tension is delicious."

"Plus there's a sexy girl on the cover," Noah adds, "just in case mystery, twists and romance aren't your thing."

"But they will be. Trust me. You should read this book."

"You should *look* at this book," Noah says. "I'm about to start drooling over it, that's how amazing the cover is."

I look at him. "Please don't drool on my book. That's gross."

"Well, not *real* drool. Like figurative drool."

"Figurative drool?"

And then we're both laughing, and instead of picking up the remote I manage to knock it onto the floor and have to crawl under my bed to fetch it, during which time Noah says, "Is she like this all the time? This is really unprofessional. Crawling under beds. Honestly. I thought we were all serious book lovers here, but—"

I jump up and push him off the bed. "And that's all we have time for today," I say with a wide grin while Noah shouts from the floor, "Help! The cushions are attacking me!"

I stop the recording, then toss a few more cushions on top of Noah, laughing the whole time. "I knew there was a reason I kept so many cushions on my bed."

"Okay, okay. You've had your fun." He pushes all the cushions away and sits up. "Now what? Do you edit the video or something? Cut the embarrassing bits? Because I happen to feel that that video is *perfect* just the way it is."

"You know what? I think I actually agree with you." I remove the memory card from the camera and slide it into my laptop. "I do still need to add some stuff to it, though. I've got this little intro video with a jingle and my photo and the words 'Andi's Book Reviews.' So that needs to go at the beginning. And there's also a thing I put at the end of all my videos that has the URLs to my Twitter, Facebook, blog and Etsy store."

"Cool. Well, you'll have to change the intro video to say 'Andi and Noah's Book Reviews.'"

"Oh will I?"

"Of course." Noah sits on the edge of my bed. "You know this isn't going to be a once-off thing, Andi. The fans will love me, and they'll be demanding more videos featuring me. You may as well make an intro that features both of us."

I shake my head, but I'm smiling, thinking to myself, *Why not?* This was the most fun I've had with a book review in a long time, so I'm probably going to ask him to help with another one. May as well make a new intro video now. "Fine. Okay, I need a picture of you." I raise my phone and snap a picture of him just as he pulls a weird face. "Fantastic. This will do perfectly."

"Wait, wait." He stands and looks at the picture over my shoulder. "I think I should pose. Maybe take my shirt off. What's the point in having all these muscles if I can't show them off to the world wide web?"

I push him back onto the bed. "You're on Facebook, aren't you? You can show your muscles off there. I don't have space for them in my videos. The only hot guys featured on my channel are the ones on book covers."

"Well, well, well." He leans back on his elbows. "Did Andrea Clark just call me hot?"

"Oops. Looks like I just did that thing where my mouth says words without letting my brain process them first.

Hang on a sec." I pause as I look over at him. "Yeah, sorry, now that my brain's caught up, I can see you're actually not that hot."

"Oh well." He stands up and pulls the old armchair across the room so it's next to my desk. "I guess Book Cover Model isn't in my future after all."

"Guess not," I say, being careful to keep my real opinion to myself this time. I haven't seen Noah without a shirt, but I'm guessing he'd make an excellent model for the kinds of books that feature manly, muscular chests on the front.

I spend the rest of the evening making a new intro video—with a lot of unhelpful advice from Noah—and then adding it to the beginning of the book review we filmed. "Cool," I say when it's done. "I'll upload it next Tuesday and send you the link. What's your email address?" I create a new contact on my phone, filling in Noah's email address and phone number and adding the picture I took of him earlier.

"Okay, that," Noah says, "I have to watch."

I look up from my phone and find him pointing to the thumbnail of one of my videos from last year. In it, I'm wearing an orange feather boa, a witch's hat, and vampire teeth. Last year's Halloween book review. "Yeah, um … no you don't."

"I do. I definitely need to watch that." He clicks the video.

"No, wait, it's not really—"

"Look, I'm gonna watch it anyway, whether now or later

on my phone. Your videos aren't exactly private, Andi."

I groan and flop onto the bed, waiting for the part where I start dancing around and chanting from the ghostly paranormal book I read for Halloween last year. Noah just about kills himself laughing, and then he watches another one of my videos. And then a few more.

"Okay, that's *definitely* enough," I say, standing up and snapping my laptop lid shut after Noah's been through at least ten of my videos. "I think you need to leave now, or I'll—Oh, crap." I squint at my phone. "Noah!"

"What?"

"It's after midnight."

"So?"

"So you can't be in here. You were supposed to leave—" I check my phone again "—fifty minutes ago. Why didn't we hear the warning beeps through the intercom?"

"Perhaps because we were laughing at you embarrassing yourself on YouTube?"

"Ugh, this is a disaster." I tug at my hair and pace the floor.

"Why? I'll just leave now."

"NO!" I push him back into the chair as he attempts to stand. "You can't leave now. If someone sees you, I'll be in trouble."

"I'll leave on my own then. No one will know I was here visiting you. I came in during dinner, so it's not like I had to sign in or anything."

"You can't leave on your own, dumbass. I have to swipe

you out. The main door will be closed now."

"Dumbass. Jeez." Noah pretends to be shocked. "Such language."

"You are *not* helping. Now you have to stay here all night, and what if there's a fire drill?"

"Look, when there's a fire drill at Smuts, there are often more girls who run outside than guys. It's not a big deal."

"Maybe not for Smuts, but it's a big deal here. What if I have to have a disciplinary hearing or something?"

"Okay, so what's your plan?"

"Um … you can …" I can't believe I'm about to suggest this. "You'll have to stay here. But you must be quiet."

"Andi." Noah sits back with a self-satisfied smirk on his face. "If you wanted me to stay the night, you should have just asked."

"Oh, shut up. You're getting a pile of cushions on the floor, and that's it."

"Five star service," Noah says. "Just the way I like it."

I throw a pillow and a whole load of cushions at him and leave him to arrange them on the floor while I tiptoe to the bathroom to change into my pyjamas. When I return, his shoes are off, but he's still wearing his tracksuit pants and T-shirt. Thank goodness. I was afraid he might strip down to boxers and nothing else. That's if he even wears boxers. He could be a briefs kinda guy.

Oh my gosh, Andi. Stop thinking about his underwear!

The cushions are laid out in a rectangle on the floor, but he's eyeing them doubtfully. I can't say I blame him. There's no way those cushions are going to stay together. "Here, put a blanket over them." I open my cupboard and pull my largest blanket down from the top shelf. "You can tuck it underneath to keep the cushions together."

I perch on the edge of my bed, putting off the inevitable awkward moment where we'll both be lying down. In the same room. Trying to sleep. Because despite the fact that it's late—very, very late—sleep isn't going to come easily to me AT ALL knowing there's a guy lying on my floor.

Noah picks up *The Italian Hoax* and lies down on his lumpy DIY mattress.

"Uh, what are you doing with that?" I ask.

"Well, I have to read it now."

"Seriously? You're gonna read that book?"

"Why wouldn't I? You told eight hundred plus subscribers how amazing it is."

"Yes. It is amazing. If it's your thing."

"And you don't think it's my thing?"

"Oh come on. Look at you." I gesture towards him. "You probably gym five hours a day while listening to rap music before jumping onto your motorbike and riding past pretty girls to show off your toned arms. Now you're telling me you want to read a paranormal mystery romance?"

He rolls onto his side and raises himself up on one elbow. "How quick you are to place me in a box. I'm offended."

"No you're not."

"Fine. I'm not. But I'm still reading the book." He lies on his back and turns to the first page. I climb beneath my duvet and lie down. "And by the way," he adds without looking up, "I don't listen to rap music. Well, I listen to some of it, but I listen to a whole lot of other stuff too."

I smile to myself. I turn off my lamp, but leave the fairy lights on so he can keep reading.

"Oh, don't worry," he says. "You can turn off the lights. I'll read by the romantic lighting of my cell phone."

"Oh, are you sure? I don't mind leaving them on."

"I'm sure. Unless you'd rather have them on." He looks up at me. "Are you afraid of the dark, Andi?"

I lean down and yank the fairy light plug out of the extension cord under my bed. "No. I am not afraid of the dark."

His cell phone light appears as he chuckles. "Good night, Andi."

"Night, Noah." I turn over and face the wall. I adjust my pillow. I tug the duvet up, pull it over me, and wiggle around until I'm comfortable. I close my eyes. And then I spend a long time listening to the quiet turning of pages before I eventually fall asleep.

"ANDI? ANDI!" LIVI SNAPS HER FINGERS IN FRONT OF MY face.

I blink. "I'm sorry, what? Were you saying something?"

"No, *you* were saying something."

"Oh. I'm sorry, I'm just really tired. I got to bed waaaaay too late last night." And I was woken way too early when a cushion flew across the room and hit my face. Well, it was after 8 am, but it felt way too early. Noah had already put the blanket away and piled the cushions onto the armchair. He said goodbye and left—with *The Italian Hoax* under his arm—and I lay in bed for a while in a half-asleep zombie state.

Then I woke up fifteen minutes before I was supposed to meet Livi, and my car wouldn't start, and Damien wouldn't answer his phone, and I ended up asking Noah for a lift—because I forgot that he doesn't have a car. He has a motorbike. And that wasn't awkward AT ALL.

Not.

I sat with my arms around his waist and my chest pressed against his back, trying not to cling too tightly to his muscled form every time we swerved around a bend. "Got a good grip there, hey?" he joked as we stopped at a traffic light. I could do nothing but laugh breathlessly and tell myself to imagine Damien instead. Damien, Damien, Damien. After all, he's the one I want to wrap my arms around, right?

"Andi?" Livi waves her hand in front of me. "I think you're doing it again."

I yawn and mumble, "I'm sorry." I look around Caffeen, the coffee shop I finished videoing just now, and wave to the nearest waitress. I need coffee. Immediately.

The waitress hurries over, and I ask her to get me the biggest, strongest mug of coffee she can find. She smiles and tells me she'll do her best to fulfil the mission.

"I, on the other hand," Livi says, "don't like coffee. What do you recommend?"

"I really like the milkshakes," the waitress says.

"Great. Um ..." Livi examines the menu. "That one please," she says, pointing. With a nod, the waitress leaves. Livi turns back to me. "So, what were you saying?"

"Um, I was saying ..." What was I saying before my mind drifted back to that motorbike ride? "Oh, I was saying that I have to tell Noah how I really feel about him."

Livi frowns. "Who's Noah?"

"Noah? Sorry, I mean Damien." I shake my head as

embarrassment heats my face. "You see? I shouldn't open my mouth until I've got caffeine in my system."

"Oh, yay, you're going to tell him!" Livi claps her hands together. "That's so exciting."

"Yes. I just keep thinking, what if I don't, and something happens, and then it's too late?"

"You mean liiiiike … maybe he elopes with a random girl he meets because he thinks you'll never love him, and only after he's married, he finds out that you do?"

"Well, probably not like that, but that sort of idea."

"You know what else falls into that sort of idea?"

"What?"

She hesitates, then says, "Not talking to your mom, and then maybe one day it's too late."

I sigh. "You know I don't want to talk about my—"

"Yeah, yeah. I know. I just keep trying in case maybe one day you do."

"Okay." I smack my hands on the table. "I'm going to do it. I'm going to tell him tonight."

"Woohoo!"

"Yes!" I pump my fist in the air, trying to get my excitement level to match Livi's. Somehow, though—probably because I'm overtired—I can't.

After a nap on Saturday afternoon, I'm ready to tell Damien. At least, I think I am. I'm supposed to be walking to Smuts just now to see him, but I'm so nervous I think I might throw up. Imagine that. *Damien, I need to tell you I've always— Oh! Bring a bucket! Quickly!*

I open my cupboard and examine my appearance once more. I'm wearing a white and grey patterned dress over sky blue tights with green gumboots. The gumboots are new, and I've been waiting for a rainy day to try them out. I'll have to put a raincoat over my dress, but that's okay. I've got a really cute one with blue and green polka dots that will be perfect for this outfit. The finishing touches are my earrings, which each have a tiny book dangling from them, and the *i carry your heart(i carry it in my heart)* pendant around my neck.

Damien likes my quirky style, so I bet he'll love this outfit.

Okay. Time to do this. I pull on the raincoat, grab my keys, and open the door. Just outside, I find Noah with his hand raised as if about to knock. "Hey." He holds up *The Italian Hoax*. "Just wanted to return your book."

"Oh." An image of him lying on my bedroom floor reading flashes across my mind. I blink it away. "You finished it already?"

"Yip. You can get a lot of reading done when you only need about four hours of sleep a night. Just imagine the possibilities, Andi." He walks in and leaves the book on my desk.

"Oh, I have. I've even tried it a few times. Always winds up with me walking around like a grumpy zombie the next day." *A little bit like today, actually.* I hang my keys on the doorknob. "What did you think of the book?" I ask, grasping at the opportunity to put off my terrifying little speech for another few minutes.

"It was pretty good," Noah says, nodding. "I enjoyed it more than I thought I would. Even the romantic tension, which was almost as *delicious* as you said it would be." He winks.

"Yes, well, I'm a girl. I enjoyed that part."

"I found the love triangle quite interesting," he adds, leaning against my desk.

"Oh yeah?"

"Yes. Now, I missed the first two books, so I just want to check something. The heroine spends most of all three books wanting to be with her investigator partner dude, right?"

"Yes."

"And finally, near the end of book three, she realises she's been chasing an idea rather than a person."

"Yes."

"And he was never the right guy for her."

"Correct."

"So essentially … this heroine is you."

"W-what?" My hand slips off the doorknob.

"Well, you've been chasing after Damien for years, haven't you? Whatever it is that you liked about him back when you were, I don't know, *ten*, probably doesn't make sense anymore."

"But … that …" How dare he come in here and tell me my life and motivations can be summed up as easily as a character's in a book? Especially when I'm about to go and bare my soul to Damien. I cross my arms tightly over my colourful raincoat. "That doesn't make sense, Noah. I'm still me and he's still Damien, so why would it matter that we're older now? And what gives you the right to say he's not the one for me? What the hell do you know?"

Noah raises his hands. "I'm not trying to make you angry, Andi. I'm trying to get you to see the truth."

"What truth? There's no hidden truth here. I love Damien and want to be with him. It's as simple as that."

"No you don't. You love the idea that he can give you the perfect life your mother never gave you."

A match strikes. Fire comes to life. "Don't you *dare* bring my mother into this. You don't know *anything* about our situation."

"I may not know everything, but I know enough from your bitter comments and all the things you won't say."

I squeeze my eyes shut and pinch the bridge of my nose with my thumb and forefinger. My limited hours of sleep are catching up to me, bringing on a headache made worse by the angry throb of blood through my veins.

"I know you don't like talking about her," Noah says, his voice gentler now, "but it isn't healthy to keep everything bottled—"

"Not healthy?" I drop my hand. "You know what's *not healthy*? Knowing that you were never wanted by either of your parents. Knowing that your father's spent his life trying to hide your existence. Knowing that your mother tried to use you as a bargaining chip to get a married man to leave his family, and when it didn't work, she almost *got rid of you.*"

Noah's expression changes. "She …"

"Yes," I say, blinking tears away. "How's that for healthy? Knowing your life was almost ended before it even began."

"But that didn't happen. You're here, Andi."

"Only because she was too much of a coward to go through with an abortion!" I shout. "And you know what else isn't healthy, Noah? Growing up without a dad. Without siblings. With a mom who went out with a different guy every weekend because none of them could ever match up to that one guy she couldn't have. Being this small, lonely, *half* family. That's not the way it's supposed to be."

"I know."

"And I am *not* going to end up like her." I swipe angrily at a tear that managed to escape. "She messed up. She didn't get anything she wanted out of life, and now she's on her own. *I don't want that.* I want …" *Dammit, tears, GO AWAY!* "I want what Damien's parents have. They're always happy. I can see how much they love each other. Whenever I visit them, I feel safe. Secure. They have what I've always wanted. The perfect family."

"Andi," Noah says gently, "there is no perfect family. If that's the only side of them you ever see, then they're hiding the bad stuff."

"What bad stuff? Why do you have to be so negative?"

"I don't mean *bad* stuff, I mean …" He pushes away from the desk, sighing in frustration. "Everyone loses their temper. Everyone gets angry. Everyone makes mistakes. At some point, everyone you love will hurt you or let you down. Will they do it intentionally? Probably not. Does it mean they don't love you? No. It just means they're human. And that's okay. That's what I'm trying to say, Andi. Life isn't perfect, *and that's okay.*"

"No it isn't! I don't want that!"

Noah watches me, then slowly folds his arms over his chest. "Then you're deluding yourself. You're hanging onto this idea of the perfect family that you've had since you were little, and you're pinning all your hopes on one person, hoping he can make everything come true. And you know what? You're probably going to wind up disappointed."

I push my door open as wide as it will go and press my back against it. "Get out of my room."

"Andi …"

"GET OUT!"

He walks past me, and I slam the door shut after him. Who the freaking heck does he think he is coming in here and telling me all that crap? He barely knows me, and he sure as hell doesn't know Damien like I do.

I march across the room, pull out several drawers of craft supplies, and dump them on the floor. I remove my gumboots and sit cross-legged in the middle of everything. Miniature books. That's what I'll make. I can use them later for necklaces or charm bracelets or key rings or … something. I need that container with all the tiny pages I cut out one afternoon while catching up on episodes of *Game of Thrones*. And leather. I need to cut leather into rectangles to wrap around the pages to form the book cover. I'll stitch the cover and pages together, then tie a leather cord around the book to hold it closed.

I should set a timer on my phone and see how long it takes me to make each little book. I've estimated before, but it might be helpful to get a more exact—

Ugh, how could Noah say that Damien isn't right for me? How could he suggest that all this time I've simply been in love with an *idea* of happiness rather than with Damien himself? Clearly he doesn't have a clue what he's talking about. Who does he think he is? Some kind of amateur psy—

Stop thinking about that, Andi!

The leather. Cut the leather into little rectangles. Try to make them all the same size. Gather a small pile of papers. Place a leather strip on top of the papers and fold the whole lot in half. Thread the needle. Push the needle through both the leather and the—

My mother didn't want a child. She wanted my dad. But he ended things with her because he came to his senses and remembered he already had a family. Then she found out she was pregnant and thought she could use it to lure him back. It didn't work. She was left alone and pregnant. She didn't want that child. She wanted to get rid of it. She wanted to have an abortion, but she was too scared. So I was born to a mother who wished I didn't exist. I've always been—

"Stop it!" I say out loud.

I drop the tiny book onto the floor and stand up. Focusing on my crafts usually helps to soothe and distract my mind, but it isn't working this time. I slip my feet back into my gumboots and cross the room to the door. I'll go out into the rain. I'll walk and walk and walk until I've pushed this afternoon so far back into my mind I'll never remember—

"No," I mutter, swinging around before my hand touches the doorknob. I walk back and drop into my desk chair. I open my laptop and log into Skype. I click my mom's name. My breathing quickens as the dialling tone sounds. She'd better answer. This is her last chance. If she doesn't—

The dialling tone stops. A second or two later, Mom appears on the screen, leaning over her computer as if she hit the answer button before even sitting down. She pulls her chair out and slides into it while saying, "Andi, darling, it's so wonderful to—

"Make me understand," I say. "Make me understand why you did everything you did. You knew he was married. Why did you ever start a relationship with him? Did you get pregnant on purpose in the hopes that he'd leave his wife? And if you honestly didn't want me, why didn't you go through with the abortion? Or put me up for adoption? And why the bloody hell did you think it was a good idea to *tell me* you ever considered an abortion? Because I could seriously have done without knowing that bit."

"Andi." She gives me a helpless look while running her

fingers through her grey-blonde hair. "Baby, I've told you so many times how grateful I am that I never went through with that. I wish I could explain how much I love you, but I don't know if it's a good idea to bring up all that—"

"You'd better try," I say, "or this will be the last conversation we ever have."

"I MET HIM AT A PARTY AT MY FRIEND JUNE'S HOUSE," MOM says. "I'd done some interior decorating for her when she first bought the house years before, and somehow we ended up friends. The party was for her work colleagues, but she invited me because one of them was single, and she thought I might hit it off with him. I didn't. I ended up spending the entire evening talking to Martin. I remember telling him how much I enjoyed his company and that his wife was a lucky woman. I never planned for it to be anything more than that.

"He travelled to Joburg a lot, so we ended up seeing more of each other over the months that followed. When we eventually … ended up together, it wasn't something either of us planned. I felt terribly guilty about it, but there was also a part of me that believed he was the right one for me and that he'd simply ended up marrying the wrong person. I secretly hoped he would come to the same realisation at some point and leave his wife. And I know—I KNOW—how wrong it was to wish for that. But I was in love, and I managed to justify my thoughts and actions.

"When he ended it, I was heartbroken. Deep down, I knew he was doing the right thing, but I was still crushed with grief. A few weeks later, when I found out I was pregnant, it was like the sun coming out after weeks of heavy clouds pressing down on me. I thought there was hope. I thought it was a sign we were meant to be together.

"Martin didn't see it that way. He told me he already had a family and didn't need another one. He said it was my decision to keep you or not, and that he'd help out financially either way. I decided that if I couldn't have Martin, then I wanted to move on completely. I didn't want to be reminded of him in any way. I looked into—" her voice wavers "—getting an abortion. But in the end, I couldn't go through with it. I couldn't end the life of my own child.

"And I have not regretted that decision, Andi. Not for a moment. You're beautiful and talented and kind and a more wonderful daughter than I could ever have asked for. I can't imagine my life without you in it." Tears slide down her cheeks. They slide down mine. "And I wish I could take back the moment when I told you what I almost did. But I was so angry when I found out you'd been through my things and contacted Martin. I know our life wasn't perfect, but I was happy with just the two of us, and I thought you were happy too. Then you told me what you'd done and that his wife and daughter now knew about us, and I was angry that you might have ruined their family and angry that I'd ever let any of this happen in the first place. You were shouting at me, demanding to know everything, and I was shouting at you, and somehow the almost-abortion ended up being one of the things that came out.

"I'm sorry, baby. I'm so sorry it was something I considered. But since the moment I decided not to do it, you have been wanted. Don't ever believe anything else."

I nod slowly, sniffing and wiping tears from my cheeks. I think I believe her. I *want* to believe her. I just need a little more time. "Um … I need to go now, Mom."

"No, Andi, please talk to me. Are you still mad at me? What can I—"

"Please, Mom. I'll … I promise I'll call you later."

I end the call and stand up. I leave my room and walk out of Fuller. Across the parking lot, down the stairs, onto the rugby field. I walk around it. Around and around. Right foot, left foot, right foot, left foot. The rain is nothing more than a drizzle, and my hood keeps my head dry.

I walk and walk and walk. And I remember. I remember Mom reading to me every night until I learned how to read to myself. I remember standing on a stool in the kitchen helping her bake. I remember the two of us sitting in front of a computer trying to figure out how to do my homework because she didn't know enough to show me what to do, but she wasn't going to give up without trying. I remember her teaching me how to use a sewing machine. Teaching me never to worry about what other people think and to be friendly rather than fighting back.

I've spent so much of the past year focused on everything Mom did wrong and the idea that I was nothing more than an inconvenient accident, that I forgot about the things she did right. And there were a lot of those things.

I climb the stairs, lean against mem stone, and search for Mom's name on my phone. After touching the call button, I tuck the phone beneath my raincoat hood and wait for her to answer.

Four rings, and then I hear her voice. "Andi?"

I bite my lip and wait a few moments for the tightness at the back of my throat to release. When I can speak, I say, "I love you, Mom."

I hear a sniff on the other end of the line. "Oh, I love you too, baby."

"I'm sorry I've been so mad at you. You've been a great mom, and I shouldn't have forgotten that just because of the things I found out last year."

"And I'm sorry I was so angry when you told me you contacted your father," she says. "I shouldn't have responded the way I did."

I nod, even though I know she can't see me. I wipe a tear from my cheek. "Mom, do you think ... do you think there's such a thing as a perfect family? Or do you think that even when two people love each other and get married and have meaningful jobs and enough money and their children are planned and everything works out the way it's supposed to, do you think even then they do stupid things and mess up what they've got and hurt people?"

"Oh, of course," Mom says. "I always used to look at Damien's parents and wish I had a marriage like theirs. It seemed perfect. But when Laura told me why they were moving to Simon's Town, I was shocked."

I frown. "What do you mean? I thought they moved to be closer to Damien."

"Oh, well that was another reason, of course." She hesitates. "I'm sorry, I thought you and Damien talked about everything. I assumed he would have mentioned why his parents moved, but if he didn't say anything, then I shouldn't either."

"Um … okay." I know she's right not to elaborate if it's something confidential, but that doesn't mean I'm not dying to know what she's talking about. And why didn't Damien say anything? He's always talked about his parents as if they're the most annoyingly happy couple in the world.

"The point is," Mom says, "to an outsider, anything can look perfect. I imagine most things aren't, though. We all make mistakes."

"Yeah. And then we say sorry."

"Yes. We say sorry, and we still love each other, and we move on."

I'M EXHAUSTED BUT I CAN'T SLEEP—A PROBLEM THAT'S new to me—which is how I find myself sitting outside on mem stone a little after 3 am on Sunday morning. Campus crime statistics run through my head, and I wonder if I'm being stupid sitting out here. A minute or two after that thought, a security guard strolls past on Rugby Road, so I pull my blanket tighter around my shoulders and don't bother going back inside.

I'm trying to come up with reasons why I love Damien, and it's proving to be harder than I thought. Is it Damien I want, or the idea that with him I'll be happy and secure? If it had been someone else with a kind, loving family who'd moved next door and been a good friend to me, would I be just as 'in love' with him as I think I am with Damien?

I try to imagine my life without him. He used to be the only one I'd confide in about anything serious, but now I've got Livi and—more recently—Carmen. I'd miss our text message exchanges. I'd miss simply being around him. I'd miss dinner with his family—which somehow reminds me of having dinner with Noah's family. 'Bring on the most boring couple of the year,' he said. I can't help smiling. Maybe Damien and I would be completely boring. I've spent so much time dreaming about the point when he'd *finally* notice me and *finally* kiss me and we'd *finally* get together, that I never considered what we'd actually be like as a couple.

He's not right for you.

I don't sense the thought forming. All of a sudden it's simply there, as though it were a sign hanging in a dark room whose light I never bothered to turn on until now. I examine the thought and find that it doesn't hurt as much as I thought it would.

He's not right for you.

Perhaps he isn't. Perhaps we were only ever meant to be friends. Perhaps there's someone a whole lot better waiting out there for me.

I drop my head into my hands and massage my temples. My head aches. I can barely keep my eyes open. Perhaps I'm tired enough now to sleep. I climb off mem stone and pull the blanket around my shoulders. Behind me, a noise disturbs the silence. I swing around, my heart speeding up and causing my head to ache even more. But it's only someone closing the door to Smuts.

The someone stands outside Smuts and does a few stretches. Then he jogs towards me. He's about to run past when he stops and says, "Andi? What are you doing out here?"

"Mike?" I take in his running shoes, shorts and T-shirt. "Okay, when you said you exercise early in the morning, I didn't realise you meant—" I check the time on my phone "—4 am."

"Yeah, I like to get a head start on days when I need to study. Running wakes me up and gets the blood pumping to my brain. Helps me concentrate better."

"On a *Sunday*?"

"Yeah, well, test tomorrow. I haven't done any work for it yet. I generally do no studying at all until the day before a test or exam—then I do a LOT of studying in one day."

"Uh huh."

"Are you okay? Why are you out here?"

"Um ... couldn't sleep."

"Oh. Well, if you want to go change, I'll wait here and you can join me for an early morning run."

An early morning run? Is he insane? "That's not gonna happen."

He laughs. "Cool, well, I'll see you around." He pauses, then adds, "Hey, can I ask you something?"

"Sure."

"You and Damien ... You're happy with him, right?"

My facial muscles manage to find the energy to frown. "Why?"

"Well, it probably isn't my place to say—"

"Probably not."

"—but sometimes you guys seem kind of ... forced

when you're together. As if it doesn't come naturally to you. I was thinking … maybe he's not the guy for you?"

I'm not sure how long my mouth hangs open before I respond. "And … you think you are?"

"Oh, no, don't worry." Mike laughs. "I'm not interested in you."

"Um. Okay." I feel the frown returning. "Are you—"

"Anyway, I've gotta get going. Enjoy sleeping in." He jogs down the stairs below mem stone and disappears.

"What the …" I murmur. That was one of the weirdest conversations I've ever had. Yet another reason I shouldn't be awake at 4 am.

I stagger back to F flat and manage to write a note to Carmen, which I stick on my door.

Please don't wake me for breakfast. Bad night. Didn't sleep.
No, I didn't tell Damien what I was going to tell him. Chat to
you later.

By lunch time on Sunday, I'm showered and dressed and ready to face the world. I need to tell Carmen what I've decided, I need to tell Damien this fake relationship has to stop, and I need to apologise to Noah for getting so upset with him yesterday. Some people hate it when they're proven wrong; I, on the other hand, am strangely excited to tell Noah he was right about Damien not being the guy for me.

I meet Carmen in the lunch queue, and she hands me a tray. Noah walks past with Yashen and another guy I don't know, and I reach out and grab his arm. He looks around, his expression becoming wary when he see it's me. "I'm sorry about yesterday," I say quickly. "For shouting at you and … all that." I let go of his arm, and he steps closer. "You, um, you were actually right. And I spoke to my mom yesterday."

Noah smiles. "Andi, that's great."

"Yeah, anyway, I'll chat to you later?" I say as the queue moves forwards.

"Yes, sure."

Carmen and I wait for our plates of res-version-of-Sunday-roast before finding a spot to sit down. I tell her about my argument with Noah, the conversation with my mom, and what I realised in the early hours of this morning. "Sounds good to me," she says when I'm done. "If you've decided that's the right thing to do, then that's great."

"Well, I think I have. I hope I'm doing the right thing. I mean, I've wanted to be with him for so long, I hope I'm not making a mistake walking away from that possibility now."

"Andi," Carmen says with a sigh, "just make up your mind. Do you want to be with the guy or not? Oh, man, is that a feather?" She pokes at her roast chicken.

"Ew. I think it is." I examine my own piece of chicken for feathers.

"Hey," Kimmy says, sitting down next to Carmen. "You know Georgia and I are watching Lumo Fox play at Kirstenbosch this afternoon? We have two spare tickets. Want to go?"

"Sure," Carmen says. "If I haven't died of food poisoning by then."

"And you, Andi?" Carmen must have told Kimmy and Georgia she was wrong about my lying, cheating ways because they're once again talking to me.

"Oh, well, I need to talk to Damien …"

"Tell him to come too. He can probably get a ticket there."

"Okay." Perhaps it's better if I tell Damien while we're in a public setting. Then we can have a pretend argument in front of a bunch of people we know so word gets around quickly that we're no longer together.

I pick up my phone from my tray and type a message.

Andi: Going to Kirstenbosch to watch Lumo Fox this afternoon. Want to come? You can get a ticket there.

Damien: A few of my friends are actually going, so that'll be cool. I'll see you there.

The parking lot at Kirstenbosch National Botanical Garden is packed. I climb out of Kimmy's car along with Carmen and Georgia, and the four of us join the crowd slowly making its way through the gardens to the concert lawn. I've got a blanket tucked under each arm, and Georgia's carrying a basket of food.

The concert lawn is more than half full already. We find a space as close to the stage as we can get, lay our blankets out, and sit down. I check my phone for messages from Damien and find that he's already here. Makes sense, I suppose. We had to wait far too long for Kimmy to finish her makeup.

"I'm going to find Damien," I tell the others, standing up and smoothing out my dress. My phone rings, and Damien's picture comes up. "Hey, I'm coming to find you," I say to him.

"I saw you stand up," he says. "Come up the hill towards the tree on your right. I'm wearing a green T-shirt."

"Oh, I see you." I wave at him and end the call. I move quickly up the hill, stepping carefully between groups of people, trying not to stand on anyone's blankets or fingers. When I reach him, he pulls me into a hug and brushes a kiss against my ear. It sends tingles through me, and I wonder yet again if I'm about to make a mistake. Maybe I shouldn't tell him to end our pretend relationship. Maybe I should instead tell him the *complete* truth, that I can't figure out how I feel about him anymore, and maybe we should test out a real relationship by going on a date.

"You look really pretty," Damien says.

"Thanks." My vintage dress has a light blue denim top with short puff sleeves, a wide brown belt, and a multi-layered, flared skirt made from soft, cream fabric. It's the kind of dress that makes me want to spin in circles.

"You can't go anywhere without pinning something to your clothes, can you?" he adds, smiling at my *Certified Book Hoarder* pin badge.

"Well, you know, I do kinda have a pin badge addiction. And a cushion addiction," I add, smiling at the thought of Noah on my floor being 'attacked' by cushions.

"And a book addiction. And possibly a YouTube addiction."

"Perhaps I have an addictive personality. I should stay away from alcohol and drugs."

"Yeah," Damien says, laughing. "Tell Livi to give up on trying to get you to drink wine."

I smile. "Anyway. Um, do you want to go for a walk quickly? I want to talk to you about something."

"Yes, of course." He puts an arm around me and leads me away from the stage towards the top of the concert lawn. "Have you seen the Tree Canopy Walkway?"

"No, I haven't been here before."

"Cool, let's go there. It shouldn't be too busy now with the concert starting soon."

"You said 'canopy,' right? Does that mean it's high? You know how I feel about heights."

"Don't worry, it's a wide walkway." He runs a hand comfortingly up and down my arm. "You'll be fine."

"Okay. Oh, can you keep my phone for me? I didn't bring a bag, and I don't have any pockets." My phone pings as I'm about to hand it over to Damien.

Noah: Found a new outfit for you ;)

Seconds later, a picture arrives of a girl wearing a dress made of pieced-together comic book pages. I laugh as I zoom in to get a better look, knowing immediately that this *has* to be my next project.

Andi: Careful. You joke, but I look at that and think, 'Awesome! Challenge accepted!'

Noah: Who says I'm joking? You could rock the comic book look.

Andi: Then it's settled. Next time I see you, we'll be ripping pages out of comic books!

Noah: Andi, how sacrilegious of you.

"You coming?"

I look up and find Damien giving me a questioning look. "Yes, sorry." I hand him my phone, still chuckling at Noah's last message.

It isn't far to the Tree Canopy Walkway, and we keep the conversation light until we get there, discussing our lectures and friends and the latest weird comments I've received on YouTube. He doesn't mention how it's going with Marie, and I don't say anything about Mike.

"Here it is," Damien says when we reach the walkway. Like a curved, wooden bridge, it starts at ground level before snaking its way through and over the trees as the ground slopes down. I grip the railing as the distance between me and the earth increases. I instruct myself to look around and not down as the walkway widens, the trees disappear behind us, and we reach a point where we can look out across the gardens.

Beneath my feet, I feel the structure swaying ever so slightly. "Whoa," I say, freezing in place. "You didn't tell me this thing moves."

"It's fine, Andi." Damien smiles and takes my hand, even though we're out of view of anyone we know, and he has no reason to keep up our pretence. "It's supposed to move a little bit. It's built that way." He pulls me further along to where we can see even more. "Look at the view. Isn't it beautiful? The mountains up there and the gardens all around us."

I nod. *Focus on the view, Andi. Not the distance to the ground.*

Damien turns to face me. "So, what did you want to talk to me about?"

"Oh. Um …" *What do I say? What do I say?* "Okay." I force myself to meet his gaze. "The truth is, I can't do this anymore. I can't keep pretending."

He breathes out a relieved sigh, his face breaking into a smile. "I'm so glad you said that. I can't pretend either. Not when all I want is for this to be real." Then he leans closer and kisses me.

The Official Mission:

Get Marie to fall for Damien and Mike to fall for Andi.

Status: Who cares?!

Andi's Side Mission:

Get Damien to fall for Andi instead of Marie.

Status: Completed!!

I'M SO STARTLED TO FIND DAMIEN'S LIPS PRESSED AGAINST mine that it takes a few seconds for me to respond. Then my eyes close and my arms slip around his neck and I kiss him back, because no matter what I was about to say, THIS is what I've always wanted. The perfect setting, the magical moment, the guy of my dreams. I'd be INSANE not to kiss him back.

Right?

Damien pulls away, and he's breathless when he says, "I can't believe this is really happening. I was too scared to hope you might feel the same way, but you do."

"I ... I do." I slide my fingers between his. "I have for a long time."

"Really?"

"Yes." I give him a shy smile. "And I never thought you'd feel the same way."

"The night you suggested we pretend to be in a relationship, I kept thinking it was a bad idea," Damien says. "That it was wrong to lie to everyone and that it would end up ruining our friendship. I thought about it every day after that, and when Valentine's Day arrived, I'd decided to tell you we shouldn't do it. But then … I saw you." He slips his hands out of mine and gently cups my face. "You were so beautiful. Laughing and relaxed and happy. You were radiant. It was like … seeing you for the first time. And I found myself wondering why I'd never looked at you that way before. Why I'd never thought of you as … more. So I asked you onto the dance floor that night planning to tell you just that. To ask you out for real and not as a pretence. But I chickened out. I wasn't brave enough. I took the coward's way out and went ahead with this plan so at least I'd get to know what it felt like to be with you, even if it wasn't real for you."

"But it was," I murmur. *And is it still?* The voice is quiet, whispering at the back of my mind, and before I have a chance to figure out the answer, Damien is kissing me again. So I tell myself that this is the right thing. This is what I want. This is what I've always wanted.

"Wow, this place is fancy," I say to Damien as we sit down inside the restaurant. It's Monday night, and we're at the V&A Waterfront for our very first real date. I told Carmen and Livi as soon as I could last night that Damien and I are together for real now. Carmen didn't seem too excited, but Livi was thrilled. She's expecting details once our date is over.

I take a peek inside the menu and suck in a breath. Okay. This is clearly the most expensive place I've ever sat down at. I assume Damien's paying, since we're on a date and he chose this restaurant, but I still don't think I can comfortably order anything more than a starter. Good thing I have a small appetite.

Damien looks around, then examines the table decor, then reads the menu. "Okay," I say after another few moments of him not looking at me. "Can I be the one to break the ice and say that this is … a little awkward?"

He smiles and reaches across the table for my hand. "It is a little. It's still so new for me to feel this way about you. For so long you've been like … well, I won't say *sister*, because that definitely would be weird, but you've been like family. Someone who's always just *there*. Someone I've taken for granted. And now I think of you as so much more. For weeks I've been dreaming of taking you out on a real date, and now it's here and I just want it to be perfect."

Weeks? I almost laugh and tell him I've been dreaming of this for *years*, but that might freak him out a little.

"That's why I picked this place," Damien continues. "My parents have been here before and they said the food is fantastic. And the view of the harbour and mountains is amazing. If we run out of things to talk about, we can at least talk about that."

I laugh. "Let's hope we don't get to the point where we have nothing to discuss but the view."

When the well-dressed waiter returns, Damien orders a tempura prawn starter and a beef fillet main—with a fancy name I can't remember—while I decide on a salad that's neither too boring nor too expensive.

"Are you sure that's enough for you?" Damien asks.

"You know I don't eat a lot," I say, then smile as I remember Noah telling his mom and aunt about my enormous appetite and the supposedly gigantic slice of cake I ate.

"I know, that's probably why you're looking so thin."

"Oh my goodness." I roll my eyes. "Now you sound like my mother. And, just like my mother, you probably don't know that I keep a stock of food in my cupboard at res so I can survive all those long nights of studying. Trust me, I've been eating plenty."

"Good to hear." He reaches for my hand again and runs his thumb back and forth over my skin. It's weird—because it's *him*—but nice. "How are things with your mom? I mean, I know you don't like to talk about her," he adds quickly, "and if it's going to ruin our dinner, then don't worry, we can move on. I just thought I should—"

"It's fine, you can ask. Things are actually much better. Noah yelled at me about a whole lot of stuff the other night, which turned out to be quite helpful." Except for the part about Damien being the wrong guy for me. That part wasn't so helpful.

Damien frowns. "He yelled at you? I'm so sorry, that

sounds horrible. He's been a bit—"

"No, no, don't worry. It was good for me. He said all this stuff about people not being perfect and how everyone will end up hurting someone they love at some point, not because they mean to, but because they're human. I couldn't get my mom out of my head after that, so I finally spoke to her about everything."

"That's great, Andi. But it's sad that Noah had to paint such a negative picture of humanity. I hope you know that I won't ever do anything to hurt you."

"Oh, I know, I know. He wasn't trying to be negative, he was just saying that no one's perfect, you know?"

"I know. That doesn't mean we can't try, though. We should all be striving for perfection."

I nod automatically, already preparing to point out to Noah that I'm not the only one dreaming of a perfect future, but I feel a frown forming as I replay Damien's words in my head. "Wait. Really? Do you really think *perfection* is what everyone should be working towards? What about … happiness, or—"

"Yes, happiness is good too." Damien smiles at me, but his hand slides away from mine. At first I wonder if I've said something wrong, but then I realise he moved because our waiter is here with the starter. As he walks away, Damien pushes the flowery centrepiece aside and moves the plate of tempura prawns to the middle of the table. "Here, this is for both of us."

"Oh, I don't eat prawns."

"Really?" Damien looks confused. "Since when?"

"Um … forever?"

"Oh. I'm sorry. It's so weird that I don't know that about you."

"I know," I say with a chuckle. "It feels as though we should know everything about each other, having been friends for so long, but I'm sure there are lots of random things that simply never came up."

"Like prawns, apparently."

"Yeah, like prawns." I laugh to show Damien it's no big deal to me because he seems a little upset by this discovery. "Oh, you know what I heard some girls talking about earlier?" I ask, picking the first subject change that comes to mind. "The Smuts formal." I give him a sideways smile. "Apparently it isn't too far away. These girls were wondering if anyone would invite them."

Damien stops chewing and stares at me with a thoughtful expression.

Crap. I'm talking without thinking again. "I mean, not that you should feel any pressure to ask me to go with you. That's not why I mentioned it. I was just … ugh. Now I'm really making this awkward."

"No, no, that's not it. I just hadn't thought about it yet. Of course we'll go together. You're my girlfriend, Andi. For real now."

Girlfriend. I expect to feel a thrill rushing through me when he says that, but my insides don't give me the reaction I was hoping for. Perhaps, since Damien's been referring to me as his girlfriend for weeks now, I've become used to it. Even though it wasn't real until now.

I clap my hands together and add in a small squeal in an attempt to get my body to respond with the appropriate level of excitement. "It will be so much fun. I've already got this fantastic idea for a dress that's a little alternative. I was going to keep it for the Fuller formal later in the year, but since the Smuts one is first, I can do it then. You're gonna love it. It'll be totally different from the standard formal dress all the other girls will be wearing."

"Awesome," Damien says, dipping a prawn into the tiny bowl of sauce on the side of the plate. "Not *too* different, though, I hope. I know you always add something quirky and interesting to your outfits—it's one of the things I love about you—but, you know, it's a formal, so you still want to look nice."

"Of course it will look nice. Have I ever crafted an outfit that doesn't look nice?"

He smiles and shakes his head, but now I'm wondering what he really thinks of my creative wardrobe choices. "Are you sure you don't want to taste this?" he asks, gesturing to the last prawn on the plate. "It's delicious."

"Um, yes. I mean, yes, I'm sure." I fiddle with the pin badge attached to the collar of my brown and white polka-dot dress and wonder if Damien finds it strange. It's a plain circle with the words *Coffee Junkie* written in brown loopy text. I thought it was cute, but maybe to Damien it doesn't count as 'nice,' especially since we're out at a fancy restaurant.

Before I can get too concerned about the matter, Damien asks how my classes are going. Discussion of our studies keeps us busy until our main meals arrive. Then we talk about his plans for the future—which include getting a master's—the friends we used to know at school, the book I'm currently reading, his parents' vegan diet, the roomful of weed-smoking Smuts guys he found when he was on duty last week, and the noisy renovations taking place on the floor above the building he has most of his lectures in. It's nice. It's comfortable. It's … a little boring.

Dammit. Noah was right.

WE MAKE OUT IN DAMIEN'S CAR IN THE SMUTS PARKING lot. The city lights sparkle in the background, cheesy love songs play on the radio, and my heart rate rises as Damien's lips move against mine, our tongues entwine, and his fingers slide through my hair.

This is right. This is perfect. This is definitely not boring. Noah was definitely wrong.

UGH! So why am I not burning up with fiery passion? Why am I wondering who the ping on my phone two minutes ago was from? Why, for freak's sake, am I thinking about Noah instead of the guy I'm currently kissing—his best friend?

Damien's hand travels slowly up my leg, pulling my skirt up with it, and I decide it's time to stop this. I put my hand on top of his, halting his progress, and pull away from the kiss. He chuckles. "Yeah, you're right. Let's take this slowly."

I reach for the door handle, then stop. "Damien, is this … the right thing? You and me?" I dare to meet his gaze and find him looking momentarily confused.

"Yes, of course." He lifts my hand and kisses it. "I think you're just feeling weird because we've been friends for so long. You'll get used to us being together soon."

"I … okay." Maybe I will. Or maybe I need a day or two to properly think about this. "I, uh, have some work I haven't finished for tomorrow yet. Do you mind if we call it a night?"

"No, not at all, I was about to suggest the same thing." He gets out his side of the car.

Wow, my sarcastic inner voice—a voice that sounds suspiciously like Noah's—whispers to me. *Don't let that passion sweep the two of you away.*

Back in my room, I flop onto my bed with my phone and discover that the message just now was from Livi.

Livi: How'd it go?

Andi: It was nice :)

Livi: Nice? REALLY? Come on, you can do better than that. Give me details.

Details? I don't want to tell her the conversation was barely a smidgen above boring and the kissing was passionless, so I type, **Um … He took me to a fancy restaurant at the Waterfront.**

Livi: Awesome :) Did you like it?

Andi: Yes.

Livi: Smoochies?

Andi: Yes.

Livi: Bum squeeze?

I roll my eyes, then type, **Yes, both cheeks.**

Livi: Okay seriously. What happened?

I may as well get some entertainment out of this evening, so I type, **I told you. He groped my butt.**

Livi: What endearing things did he say?

Andi: "You have firm cheeks."

Livi: No, really. What did he say?

Andi: "You've obviously been working out."

Livi: Andi! Come on!

I roll onto my tummy, giggling and typing, **You saying I have flabby cheeks?**

Livi: Andrea Clark!

Andi: I'll let you have a squeeze next time I see you.

Livi: Oh. My. Hat. I give up.

Andi: *laughing*

Livi: *sighing* Fine. But you're gonna have to spill when I see you.

I put my phone down as my smile fades. If only I'd enjoyed the date as much as I enjoyed making fun of it.

"Andi, hey!" Livi says as she pulls open the door to her second-floor flat. "What are you doing here?"

"Um …" I twist my hands together. "Avoiding my new boyfriend?"

"What?" Livi's expression falls. "You guys have been together two days. Why are you avoiding him already?"

I groan as I walk past her into the flat. "Last night's date wasn't as amazing as I may have led you to believe."

"Oh, you mean with the evasive non-answers about your butt? Trust me, you didn't lead me to believe anything except that you're infuriating."

"Right. Well—Oh, hey, Adam." I wave to Livi's boyfriend who's sitting on the couch with a paused movie on the TV in front of him.

"Hey," he answers. "Uh … I'm just gonna sit here and pretend I'm not listening to you two talking about butts."

Livi rolls her eyes. "Keep watching the movie. We'll chat in my room."

I follow her past the couch and into her bedroom. She closes the door, then moves a pile of papers with music notes scribbled on them off her bed. "You've been composing?" I ask as I sit.

"Mmm, just some simple stuff. I've been avoiding studying for the past few days. And speaking of avoiding …" She gives me a pointed look.

"Yes. Damien. I'm avoiding him because I'm pretty sure we're not right together and I need to break up with him and I'm kinda scared of doing it."

Livi's eyebrows climb upward. "Are you sure? I mean, we're talking about the guy you've spent years pining after, right?"

"Right. But you know what? When I went to talk to him on Sunday, it wasn't to tell him I've always loved him. It was to tell him we needed to end our fake relationship and just be friends. I'd already decided he wasn't right for me. But then he surprised me by kissing me, and I got all confused and figured maybe it was right after all, and I just went with it."

Livi nods slowly. On the bed between us, her phone

starts playing piano music I don't recognise and the name 'Sarah' appears. Livi switches the phone to silent. "I'll call her back just now."

"Okay. So now I'm starting to think I was right the first time and that everything Noah said was, in fact, true."

"Who's Noah?"

"Um, one of Damien's friends. And my friend too, I guess. I mean, we made a video together, so we must be— ANYWAY, I'm getting sidetracked. Noah pointed out that I've been chasing after this dream of a perfect relationship rather than Damien himself. It could have been any nice guy living next door to me and I probably would have attached the same feelings to him."

Livi stares quizzically at me. "What do you mean you *made a video together?*"

"Ugh, Livi, not a *dodgy* video. A book review video. You're missing the point. The—"

"The point here is that you have a simple decision to make," Livi says. "Do you see you and Damien having a future together? Do you *really want* to have a future with him? If not, then it's simple: He's not the one for you. I mean, unless …"

"Unless what?"

"Well, if you're the kind of person who's just looking for a casual fling, then it doesn't really—"

"No, jeepers. Would I have spent years pining after this guy—or this *idea*, or whatever—if I were a casual fling kinda person?"

"Okay. Sorry." Her cell phone screen lights up as a

message comes through. She picks the phone up. "It's just that we haven't known each other that long. I had to check. And I wouldn't … judge you … if …" She stares harder at her phone, clearly losing track of whatever she was saying. "Ohmygosh." She straightens, then jumps off the bed. "Ohmygosh ohmygosh ohmygosh. Adam!" she shrieks, yanking her bedroom door open and running out. "Look look look!" She lands on the couch and shoves her phone in Adam's face.

"What? What's wrong? What happened?" He scrambles into a sitting position as I rush into the lounge to find out the same thing.

"SARAH'S GETTING MARRIED!" Livi squeals and bounces up and down. "She and Aiden just got engaged. Look at the video. Oh my hat. I think I'm gonna cry. My best friend is *getting married.*" She jumps off the couch, runs to where I'm standing, and squeezes me in a tight hug. Then she dashes back to Adam, grabs the phone, and brings it to me. "Look, it's so romantic."

She taps the screen so the video starts playing once more. The scene is of a guy and girl in the mountains somewhere with a cliff rising to their right and the beginnings of a sunset tingeing the sky that's visible on the left. Whoever's taking the video is obviously hiding, because tree branches are visible around the edges of the screen. The guy lets go of the girl's hand and gets down on one knee. The girl claps both hands over her mouth, clearly shocked. She nods, slowly, then more vigorously, and the guy stands and pulls her into an embrace. Then the video cuts to a close-up of them laughing and hugging as the girl waves the back of her hand at the camera, showing off her ring.

I feel oddly emotional as the video ends, not because I know these two people, but because the happiness I see on the screen—that pure, overflowing joy—is what I've always wanted. And I know in this moment, without a doubt, that Damien isn't the one to give me that.

23

Mandy Lovet (1 hour ago)
omg who is the hot guy?! please do more videos with
him!

Zelly (2 hours ago)
Nice to meet you, Noah. And no, Andi doesn't normally
crawl around under the bed. She's usually way more
composed in her videos!

Apple Turtle (1 hour ago)
I like the non-composed version of Andi ;)

> **Zelly** (32 min ago)
> Me too!

> **Apple Turtle** (21 min ago)
> Think somebody's got a crush on somebody?!

Chelsea L R (2 hours ago)
Cant wait to read this book but wil have 2 read it slowly
since its the last in the series :-(and thanks 4
introducing us 2 your boyfriend he seems nice :-)

Becky Becks (4 hours ago)
Hey, I'm a new subscriber! My friend recommended
your channel. Wouldn't normally read this genre, but
your review was entertaining enough to make me one-
click the ebook of the first novel in the series!

Shania Martinez (5 hours ago)
Read it already. It was great! And yes, the cover rocks ;-)

LollyMBooks (5 hours ago)
Andi, are you blushing?! LOL ;)

I sit on mem stone early in the evening on Wednesday
and laugh at all the comments on the YouTube review of
The Italian Hoax. Students walking across the parking lot and
down the stairs give me odd looks, but I'm too busy
chuckling and typing replies to be bothered. When I'm done
replying, I send Noah a message.

Andi: I posted our book review video about a day and a
half ago and it already has more views and comments
than any of my other videos :D

Noah: Told you they'd love me ;)

Andi: :P

Noah: You didn't send me the link, but I found the video quite easily. Enjoying the comments ;)

My face heats up and embarrassment curls in my stomach as I imagine Noah reading all those comments. At least, I think it's embarrassment. Ignoring the weird feeling, I slide the phone into my polka-dot raincoat—the sky looked threatening when I left my room—and watch the passing students as I wait for Damien. He said he just needed to shower quickly after his jog around campus.

"Hey, Andi."

I look up, expecting to find Damien coming towards me—quickest shower ever—but see Noah instead. "Oh, hey."

He waves his phone at me. "Latest comment says we need to make our joint book reviews a regular thing, although the commenter did say she'd like it if I actually *read* the books we review so she can get a guy's opinion of the inside and not just the cover."

"Well, now you can reply to her and say you have read it." I notice the towel around his neck and the sheen of sweat covering his bare arms and face. "Were you out running with Damien?"

"No, I was at the gym. Getting in my five hours a day while listening to rap music." I laugh as he pushes himself up onto the stone beside me. "I actually haven't seen Damien for a number of days. I guess he's been busy. How's it going with you guys?" He runs a hand over his sweaty head. "Are you, uh, still doing your pretend dating thing?"

"Um, no. We actually got together for real."

Noah drops his hand. "What?"

"Yes." Confusion furrows my brow. "Didn't Damien tell you? Don't you guys talk to each other?"

Noah looks away so I can't see his expression. "Apparently not."

"Yeah, it's kind of a funny story, actually." I swing my legs forward and back, bumping them gently against the stone. "I'd decided that Damien *wasn't* right for me, just like you said. I went to tell him we should stop pretending we're together, and he ended up kissing me and saying he wants to be with me for real. Somehow that muddled my brain and I thought maybe after all he *was* right for me. So we went out on Monday night, but then—"

"I can't believe you," Noah says, jumping off mem stone. "*Or* him." Without waiting for my reply, he turns and walks briskly back towards Smuts.

"Hey!" I yell after him. "Don't you want to hear the end of the story?"

No response. He keeps walking.

"Idiot," I mutter to myself as I hastily jump down and follow him. This is why I'm annoyed by so many chick flicks. People always end up with half the story when things would be a lot simpler if everyone knew everything. But I suppose there wouldn't be much of a story then. Well, this isn't going to turn out like those movies. I change my walk to a jog, hoping I'll catch up with Noah before he gets inside. If the silly boy had just waited another few seconds for the end of my story, he would have had no reason to get upset. And, now that I think about it, what does he have to get upset about in the first place?

I run into the Smuts foyer as the glass door with swipe-card access swings shut. "Noah!" I shout, but he either doesn't hear me or chooses not to. I bounce impatiently on my feet as I watch a guy I don't know coming towards me on the other side of the door. I'm pretty sure grass grows faster than this guy can walk.

When he eventually swipes his student card to open the door, I dart through before he can get out. Noah was moving in the opposite direction to where his flat is, so I'm pretty sure he's gone to Damien's room. I run along the corridor and up the stairs. "Oh, hey, Noah," Damien's voice says somewhere above me.

"I'm pleased to see you remember me," Noah says. "You've been avoiding me for at least a week."

I slow down, wondering if it might not be the best idea to get involved in whatever conversation is coming.

"I just discovered something that really confuses me," Noah says as I turn around on the stairs and prepare to tiptoe back down. "You and Andi are dating. For real this time. Want to know why that confuses me?"

"Look, Noah—"

"You see, I remember a conversation from not too long ago. A conversation that happened after a game of pool." I freeze on the stairs, knowing I shouldn't be listening to this but unable to make myself leave. "Remember that one?" Noah says. "Remember when I spoke to you about Andi, and you said, 'Yeah, she dresses weirdly, but other than that she is rather amazing.'"

I dress weirdly?

"And I thought you were *encouraging* me. You didn't give me any hint that you were interested in her."

"Look, I wasn't sure at that point if—"

"And what about the conversation we had *last week*, Damien?" Noah continues. "Are you choosing to conveniently forget that one too? The one where I said, 'I never thought I'd get over Tania, but I think it's finally possible.' The whole time I was talking to you about Andi, you didn't once think to tell me how you actually feel about her?"

"Yeah, well, I didn't know if she felt the same way."

"So instead you sat there saying things like, 'That's great. Good for you. You're finally moving on.' And a few days later, when Andi came to you to *end* that fake relationship and *not* start a real one, you decided to kiss her and complicate things even further."

"Hang on," Damien says. "Andi feels the same way about me, okay? That's why we're together now. She chose me. I didn't force her into anything."

Silence follows, and I wonder if Noah's about to come down the stairs and catch me here. "Well," he says eventually, his voice quieter now. "As long as it was her choice. I'm not sure where this leaves you and me, though."

"Well, if you want to end our friendship over a girl, that's up to you."

"It actually has a lot more to do with my best friend deceiving me than with the girl he's dating."

"Deceiving you? I—" Damien lets out a short laugh. "Come on, man. Don't be ridiculous. There was never any deception. And if it makes you feel better, I don't think you ever stood a chance with her. You're not exactly her type. You're …"

"I'm what?"

"Well, she's … and you're …"

"Is there something you're afraid to spit out, Damien?" Noah demands.

"Andi doesn't like coloured guys, okay? She told me she was getting a little creeped out with you hanging around her so much."

WHAT? Without thinking, I turn and march up the stairs. "How *dare* you put words into my mouth that were never there?" I shout at a startled Damien.

"I—Andi—How long have you—"

"Sure, I've never dated a coloured guy before, or a black guy or an Indian or *any* guy for that matter, because I've spent half my life hung up on you. And that doesn't make me racist, that makes me a desperate fool."

"Well," Noah says. "I'm glad you're finally accepting the truth."

"And *you*," I shout, turning to him. "You couldn't stay sitting for another *three seconds* so I could tell you that after the date Damien and I went on, I decided you were definitely right about him not being the guy for me."

"What?" Damien says. "You decided I'm not—and you—" He faces Noah. "You want to talk to *me* about deception when you've been telling her not to date me? You're a damn—"

"It wasn't like that," Noah shouts. "I wasn't trying to get her to choose me over you. I was trying to get her to see that the person she fell in love with when you were both kids doesn't exist anymore, and possibly never did."

Damien looks at me. "You … how long have you—"

"For too long, Damien. For *too long*. I've watched you with every girlfriend you've ever had, I've listened to all your problems and all your break-ups and all your musings about the next perfect girl to come along. And when it was finally my turn, I realised it was too late for us. You're not the person I need, and I'm not the person you need."

"So the fake relationship idea was a lie from the start," Damien says quietly. "You weren't doing it to help me get Marie. You were doing it so *you*'d get me. You've been deceiving me too."

"Oh my gosh, *everyone*'s been deceiving *everyone*, okay? I never liked Mike, and apparently you got over Marie pretty quickly, which means that when you were hanging out with her, you were probably only doing it to make *me* jealous instead of the other way around. We've both lied. We've both kept things secret that probably should have been said out loud. Now we need to just *stop* everything and move on."

"And what about poor Marie and Mike?" Noah says. "Are they supposed to be left wanting both of you when neither of you want them anymore?"

"You." I point at him. "Just stop. You're always going on about bottling things up and how it's not healthy and I need to get everything out, but what about you? *You* don't tell *me* anything. Who's Tania, huh? And why did you think you'd never get over her?"

Noah steps closer to me, his voice growing dangerously low as he speaks. "Perhaps if you'd taken the time to *ask* about my private life, the way I did for you, then you'd know."

"Well maybe I'm of the opinion that private lives are PRIVATE!" I yell.

"SHUT UP!"

I jump as the voice of someone I had no idea was there shouts from the stairs below me. I swivel around and look down. "Mike?" I whisper in horror.

"I came to ask my sub-warden a question about the tutoring programme," Mike says. "Guess I arrived at a bad time." And with that, he turns and disappears down the stairs, leaving me without a doubt that he heard everything he wasn't supposed to.

DAMMIT!

I hurry downstairs after him, reaching the corridor in time to see him walking briskly away. I almost chase after him, but I have no idea what I'd say. So I run for the foyer instead, tears already pricking behind my eyes.

I RUN ALL THE WAY BACK TO MY ROOM AT FULLER. I KICK my shoes off, drop my raincoat on the floor, silence my cell phone, and climb into bed. I'm glad for my numerous cushions this evening; they're helping to hide me from the world. It isn't even dark yet, but I don't care. I want to fall asleep so my brain doesn't keep replaying all our horrible, angry words. So I won't keep seeing their faces over and over. Damien's guilt when he realised I'd heard everything he said. Mike's disappointment at hearing about our scheme. And the hurt in Noah's eyes when I turned on him.

Through the duvet and cushions, I hear a soft tap on my door. "Andi?" Carmen calls to me. "Is everything okay? I heard your door slamming."

I consider ignoring her, but I've already alienated three people today. I should probably try to keep the friends I have left. I lower the duvet cover and say, "I think it's unlocked."

She opens the door and surveys me amidst my comfort-pile of cushions. "Early night?"

"You could say that."

"It didn't go well when you spoke to Damien?"

I shake my head. "The poop hit the fan. In a BIG way."

"Well, that sounds like a good story," Carmen says, shutting the door and swiping several cushions off the bed so she can sit. "Do tell."

I relate the whole messy confrontation. "I didn't even get to say the things I was planning to say to Damien," I add at the end. "All the wrong stuff spewed out, and then Mike was suddenly there, and then I ran away like a scared ostrich-chicken."

"Ostrich-chicken? Because ... you're hiding from the problem like an ostrich and you're scared like a chicken?"

"Yes. I should put that on a pin badge," I murmur, sinking further down beneath my duvet. "*Scared Ostrich-Chicken.* I'll put it on a hat so everyone will know the truth about me."

"You may be unaware of this," Carmen says, "but self-pity is very unattractive on you."

"Wow. Your bedside manner is exceptional. You should be a doctor."

"Sarcasm's right up there with self-pity."

"Ugh, come on! Just give me five minutes to wallow. I messed up, okay? Badly. They all hate me now. Damien, Noah, Mike. Marie's probably going to find out soon as well, since we were yelling loud enough for at least half of Smuts to hear us, and then she'll hate me too."

"Well … yes, I suppose they might hate you. But they'll probably get over it. And I doubt you were the only one at fault. Damien doesn't exactly have any right to hate you after he flat out lied to Noah about you."

"Yes," I say, thinking back to that part. "How could he say that? How could he tell such a horrible lie so easily to someone who's meant to be his best friend? I'd never have believed it if I hadn't heard it myself."

"I would have," Carmen mutters, looking away.

I stare at her. "Why do you say that? Do you know something?"

She sighs. "When you told me you guys got together for real, I figured I'd have to show you, but now that you've broken up, it isn't necessary for—"

"You've been keeping something from me?" I demand, sitting up. "After you ignored me for *weeks* because I did the same thing to you?"

"Okay, look." She holds her hands up. "I realise that after we had that long chat in the car about being honest, I probably should have told you this. But when I realised it wasn't actually you Damien was cheating with, I figured I didn't need to create any more drama by showing you."

"By showing me *what?*" I ask, my voice icy. "I swear, if you don't open up right now, there's gonna be a whole lot more poop flying at the fan." She stands, opens my door, and heads across the landing to her own room. Seconds later, she's back, holding something small in her hand. She holds it up. "A flash drive?" I take it from her. "Wait, is this …" The initials D. S. are written on the side. "Damien Sanders," I whisper.

"Yes," she says. "I found it outside a few days after we moved into Fuller. Then I forgot about it. When I remembered it a couple of weeks later, I figured I'd just take a quick look at it to find out who it belongs to, but I saw a little more than I bargained for."

I look up. "What's on it?"

"Perhaps you should see for yourself." She reaches for my laptop on the desk and passes it to me.

With apprehension filling my stomach, I lift the laptop lid and plug the flash drive in. It's filled with folders and documents labelled with course, assignment, and project names. There's nothing immediately suspicious. "What am I looking for?"

"A document called 'Letter.'"

I raise an eyebrow. "You opened a document called 'Letter'?"

"Well, I wasn't planning to *read* it. I thought I'd just scroll to the bottom and check for a name."

I move my finger over the touchpad until the mouse pointer is sitting over the 'Letter' file. I hesitate, then double click to open it.

When I hung up the phone just now, there were so many things I still wanted to say. So many things I told myself I shouldn't say. But I can't help it anymore. You know how I feel about

*you, and I know you feel the same, so I don't see a reason to
deny this any longer.*

I'm falling for you.

I can't stop thinking about you.

I wish I could be around you all the time.

*I live for the moments when my phone pings and I get a
message from you, and I wish I could have more. More than
just messages and phone calls late at night. I wish we could be*
real *and* out in the open.

*You asked me once before, and I told you I couldn't then. I
couldn't be with you while Charlotte was going through such a
difficult time. But I've thought about it many times, and if you
are still asking, my answer now is* yes.

Damien

I blink at the words on the screen. "He lied after all," I murmur. "He really was cheating on Charlotte."

Carmen nods. "And I assumed it was with you, which is why I thought you were lying to me. It was only after you yelled at me that I realised your name isn't anywhere in the letter and that it could have been anyone." She pauses. "Are you … okay?"

If I'd discovered this a few months ago, I'd be devastated, but after hearing Damien lie about me earlier, it isn't entirely surprising to discover he lied about this too. "Yeah. I'm okay." I snap the laptop shut and push cushions out the way so I can get up. "Doesn't mean I'm not confronting him about it."

"Oh. Um, are you—"

"Yes." I slip my feet back into my shoes.

"But what if he—"

"Still yes." I yank the flash drive from the laptop and push it into my jeans pocket.

"Andi!" she shouts in frustration. "You don't even know what I'm trying to say."

"It doesn't matter what you're trying to say." I grab my keys. "Put the latch down when you leave, will you?" I run downstairs and out of Fuller. Light rain sprinkles across my bare arms, but it doesn't matter that I left my raincoat because it only takes half a minute or so to get to Smuts. I reach it just as a large group of guys are coming out, probably on their way to dinner, which makes it easy for me to slip past them. I run up Damien's stairs and push his door open without bothering to knock—a move that would have been a bit awkward if the door had been locked.

"Andi?" Damien looks up from his desk, startled. He stands. "Andi, I'm so glad you came back. I've been calling and calling you. All that stuff about deception and lies … we can move past that, right? I … it's …"

"I thought you liked the way I dress," I say, placing my hands on my hips.

"What?" He frowns. "Yeah. I do. I've told you that before."

"But you also told Noah that I dress weirdly."

Wariness appears in Damien's eyes. "No, what I meant was that that's how some other people see you. I've never seen you that way. I like your style."

"Really. Well you know what, Damien? I don't believe you. I never would have called you a liar, but you've lied to me so many times in the past few weeks that I don't know what to believe anymore."

"Andi," he says, looking hurt. "How can you say that? What have I lied to you about?"

I pull the flash drive out of my back pocket and hold it up. "Who were you cheating on Charlotte with?"

"*What?* Andi, you know I'd never—"

"I saw the letter. I know you were still with Charlotte when you wrote it. You called her paranoid for thinking you were cheating on her, but she was right all along." I throw the flash drive at him. He fumbles, but manages to catch it.

"At the beginning of the year," he says slowly, turning the flash drive over in his hands, "the first day I saw you, I told you I'd lost this. Have you had it since then? Have you been keeping this secret to yourself all this time, waiting for a moment when you could use it against me?"

"Are you *crazy*? You might have done something like that, Damien, but not me. I saw that letter for the first time about five minutes ago because somebody who is a *real* friend to me decided I needed to see it."

"Well that *real* friend of yours needn't have bothered. I wrote that letter when I was feeling desperate, but I never sent it. Nothing ever happened with her."

"With who? Was it Marie?"

"It doesn't matter because nothing happened!"

"Why did you save the letter?"

"DEAR GOD, ANDI," Damien shouts as he flings the flash drive at the wall. "Stop being so bloody PARANOID."

I take an involuntary step backwards, feeling for a moment as though I'm standing in front of a different person. I remember Noah saying that fighting isn't bad, it's honest, and I wonder if that means I've never seen the real Damien before. I've never even seen him mildly angry, much less furious.

"Okay," I say, holding my hands up as though attempting to calm a wild animal. "I'm sorry. I suppose it's possible you could have written that letter and never sent it."

"It isn't just possible, Andi. THAT'S WHAT HAPPENED. And now, thanks to this whole mess you caused with Noah, you and I have to break up. Just like every other girl I've been with, you've managed to screw up what could have been perfect."

"I've—Wait a minute. You think every relationship you've been in ended because of something the *girl* did wrong?"

"Well," Damien says, spreading his hands out, "it wasn't due to anything I did. You said yourself you've been there for every girlfriend I've had. If I was the reason those relationships ended, why on earth would you want to be with me?"

"I don't. That's what I've been wanting to tell you since our date on Monday night. We're not right for each other."

Damien's hands clench into fists as he folds them over

his chest. "You only think that because you let Noah mess with your head. Both of you were my friends, and you both ended up deceiving me."

I want to shout at him, tell him to get over his persecution complex, but I decide there's no point. We'll simply keep going back and forth, yelling accusations and hurting each other more and more. At this rate, we'll never be friends again. "I think it's time for me to go," I say quietly. "Goodbye and … I'm sorry."

The Official Mission:

Get Marie to fall for Damien and Mike to fall for Andi.

Status: Failed. (I think. I don't actually know how Marie feels about Damien, but I highly doubt Mike ever fell for me. I'm pretty sure Damien's the one he was interested in all along …)

Andi's Side Mission:

Get Damien to fall for Andi instead of Marie.

Status: Aborted.

"THANKS SO MUCH FOR LETTING ME STAY HERE FOR A BIT," I say as I drag my suitcase through the door into Livi's flat. "I know you don't have much space." I push the suitcase behind the kitchen table where it'll be out of the way for now and leave my sewing machine on the table.

"Yeah, I'm sorry there's no guest room," Livi says, "but the couch is big and *super* comfy. Adam falls asleep on it all the time when he visits."

"Thank you. And I promise I'll fold up the blankets and things every day so they're not in your way."

"Sure, whatever. Oh, there are some shelves in the bathroom that I never got around to using, so you can keep some stuff there if you want." She plops onto the couch and crosses her legs. "This is gonna be fun," she says with a wide smile. "I know the reason you're here isn't exactly a positive one, but it'll still be fun. We can share clothes and watch movies when we should be studying and bake stuff we shouldn't be eating."

"You want to share *my* clothes? Really?" Damien's words run through my head. "You don't think they're a little … weird?"

"Well, sure, some of them are. But I'd love to borrow the less weird ones."

I blink. "Um. I'm still trying to figure out if I should be offended by the word 'weird.'"

She sighs and rolls her eyes. "Of course you shouldn't. 'Weird' was your word, not mine. I might have gone with 'funky' or 'eccentric.' Besides, who cares what you call it? You've totally pulled off every outfit I've ever seen you in, and that's all that matters. You could probably wear a dress made of pieced-together feather dusters and still look fabulous."

"You think?" I rub my chin thoughtfully. "I've never ventured into feather territory before. Always thought it seemed a bit messy."

Livi laughs. "You have the kind of confidence I've always dreamed of having. You can wear anything." She reaches for the bowl of popcorn sitting on the coffee table and offers me some. "By the way, I'm guessing you *make* a lot of your clothes, right? That's why the sewing machine's here?"

I scoop a handful of popcorn out of the bowl. "Well, it's mainly for my Etsy products—the scarves and bags and headbands and stuff—but I do make some of my clothes.

And almost everything I buy gets altered in some way." I munch on a mouthful of popcorn, then add, "Oh, I made these pants, actually." I stand up to show off my pants made from white fabric printed with a pattern of joined newspaper pages. I still remember how excited I was when I found the fabric while hunting for something to make tote bags from.

"You *made* those?" Livi says, her eyes widening in awe.

I sit down and tuck my legs beneath me. "It's not that hard. Just takes a little bit of practise. Anyone with two brain cells to rub together can figure it out."

"Yeah, maybe two of your brain cells. You should be a fashion designer, Andi."

I nod. "I think I should. Neither of my parents thought that was a viable career option, though. They said I had to get a 'sensible' degree first, and then I could do whatever I want."

"Okay, I can see Dad saying that," Livi says, "but isn't your mom an interior decorator?"

"Yes."

"So she dresses up rooms, but she isn't happy with you dressing up people?"

"Something like that."

Livi sighs. "Parents."

"I know."

She picks up the remote control and presses the play button. The movie that was paused—the latest *Star Trek*— jumps to life. "This is possibly the hundredth time I'm watching this movie," she says, "so if you want to change it to something else, or if you need to go study in my room, that's cool."

With a week and a half left of the quarter, and several tests coming up next week, I probably should be studying. I'd far rather watch *Star Trek*, though. "I'm exactly where I want to be right now. Studying can happen on the weekend."

We crunch on popcorn, and half a minute later, Livi says, "Oh, I just thought of something." She turns the volume down on the movie. "Are you going home for the Easter holidays next weekend?"

"No. Mom and I looked at flights, but they're quite pricey. Budget's kinda tight this year with my tuition and res fees."

"Isn't Dad helping?" Livi says with a frown.

"Um, yes, I think he's contributing. He and my mom came to some kind of agreement. And I've got my Etsy savings to cover living expenses. That doesn't leave much to buy plane tickets, though."

"Oh. Well I was asking because I *am* going home, and I thought maybe you'd want to stay here. You'll have the place to yourself. Cavendish Square is down the road, so you can chill at coffee shops and read, or you can stay here and watch movies all day. Whatever."

"That actually sounds amazing." I'd pictured myself hiding inside Fuller during the holidays in an attempt to avoid Damien, who isn't going home either, but staying at Livi's is a far better option.

"Great," Livi says with a smile. We turn back to the movie, but she doesn't increase the volume yet. "Sooooo," she says slowly. "Are we ever going to talk about your boy troubles?"

"Boy troubles?" I ask lightly.

She picks up her phone from the coffee table and reads out my last message to her. "'I broke up with my ex-pretend-boyfriend-now-ex-real-boyfriend. The guy I was PRETENDING to like possibly doesn't even like girls. And the only guy I still want to spend time with—my ex-pretend-boyfriend-now-ex-real-boyfriend's ex-best friend—doesn't ever want to talk to me again. Bottom line? I need to get out of res. PLEASE can I come stay with you!'"

"Ah," I say. "Those boy troubles."

I MAKE IT THROUGH THE LAST WEEK OF THE QUARTER without bumping into Damien, Noah or Mike. Damien and Mike I'm relieved about, but part of me wishes I could see Noah. I want to visit more coffee shops with him. Or record another book review video with him. Or show him the website I found that sells comic book fabric. In fact, it wouldn't really matter what we *do*, if I could just spend some time with him.

I keep myself busy during the week-long holiday. I do two coffee shop videos—one at Origin Coffee and another at Deluxe Coffeeworks—read several books, record a book review, and come up with some new items for my Etsy store. Three days before the end of the holiday, the flannel Wonder Woman fabric I ordered online arrives. I plan to make a few small items like scarves and hand warmers to sell on Etsy—to make back the cost of the fabric—but my main reason for buying this fabric was to sew a pair of winter pyjamas for myself. We're into April now, and the nights are getting colder. What better way to spend them than wrapped in cosy Wonder Woman PJs?

Well, Andi, you could spend those cold nights wrapped up in a certain guy whose name begins with—

No. I've had enough boy drama recently. Besides, I haven't heard from that certain someone since I ran out of Smuts over two weeks ago. I'm probably the last person he wants to see. Even if he has been replying to some of the comments left on our YouTube video. Not that I've been stalking his recently created YouTube account or anything.

Okay, Andi, I tell myself. *Time to sew.*

When Livi returns on Sunday evening, I'm wearing my new pyjamas. "You look so cute!" she exclaims when I open the door to let her in. "Did you make those? Please can I have some!"

"I should show you this website, actually," I tell her as she wheels her suitcase into her bedroom. "It's got *Star Trek* fabric and *Star Wars* and Marvel comics and DC comics and a whole lot of other stuff."

"Yes! Show me, show me!"

We make a bowl of popcorn and sit on the couch with my laptop so I can show Livi her options. After examining every pattern, she chooses *Star Trek*, which we both knew she was going to do from the beginning. "Now you have a birthday present for me," she says, hugging a cushion. Her intercom buzzes. "Oh, that should be Allegra and Salima." She tosses the cushion aside and stands up. "We need to finish an assignment for next week. Salima was bugging me about it the whole time I was at home."

She presses a button to let her friends in through the main door downstairs, then opens her own door. "Hello, hello!" she shouts down the stairs, then claps a hand over her mouth and looks back at me with a guilty expression. "Oops. The neighbours don't like it when I get noisy."

Allegra and Salima walk in, Salima saying, "Don't shout, Livi. You know how grouchy your neighbours can get."

"Nice to see you too, Salima," Livi says as she shuts the door.

"Hi, Andi." Allegra waves to me before heading to Livi's bedroom.

"I brought healthy snacks," Salima says, following her. "We need our brains to remain focused."

"And I brought unhealthy ones," Allegra adds.

Livi turns to me, already looking tired. "Well, this should be fun. Enjoy whatever movie you're watching tonight."

"Thanks. Enjoy your healthy snacks," I say with a grin.

She sticks her tongue out at me before disappearing into her room.

I'm half an hour into *Avatar* when there's a knock at the front door. I pause the movie as Livi leans out of her bedroom. "Is someone here?"

"I think so."

She lowers her voice and says, "Ugh, it must be a neighbour. I wonder what they're complaining about now." She walks past the back of the couch, pausing to direct my head back towards the TV. "Face forwards," she whispers.

"You don't want to get involved in whatever drama is about to go down." With a frown, I stare at the paused characters on the screen and listen to Livi opening the door. "Oh. Hi," she says. "Can I help you?"

"Yes, uh, is Andi here?"

The remote slips from my fingers at the sound of the familiar voice. It clatters onto the floor, and I dive after it.

"You must be Noah," Livi says, her smile evident in her voice. "What a pleasure to finally meet you. And yes, Andi is here." I sit up and look over the back of the couch. Livi mouths, *He's hot*, while Noah gives me an uncertain smile from over her shoulder. "Well, I've got work to carry on with, so you guys have fun." She gives me a knowing look before skipping back to her bedroom and closing the door.

I stand up, running my fingers through my hair and wondering why Noah couldn't have caught me in a slightly sexier outfit—and then wondering why I even care—than my Wonder Woman PJs, one blue sock, and one white sock. "Hi," I say.

"Hi." He takes a few steps closer to the lounge area and places his hands on the back of the couch.

"How did you get up here?"

"I was about to buzz, but someone was coming into the building and held the door open for me."

"Aaand how did you know I was here?"

"Uh, I asked Carmen. I haven't seen you around for a while, so I just wanted to check you were okay."

"I am," I say, nodding. "Are you?"

"Yes. I'm okay."

"Good."

"Great."

I pause, then add, "Is this about to become the most awkward conversation either of us has ever had?"

"Well, I don't know about you, but I think this is already the most awkward conversation I've ever had."

"I think so. Me too." My fingers fiddle with the hem of my pyjama top. "Since it's already awkward, I should probably dive right in and say I'm really sorry for that big fight outside Damien's room. I was waiting at mem stone for him to meet me so I could break up with him, but then you rushed off and confronted him and made it all into a big mess, and I got really mad at both of you, even though maybe it was good to get everything out in the open because at least we were all being honest—although I'm still not a hundred percent sure if I can believe everything Damien said, because after that, I … Jeepers, I am totally messing up this apology. I—yeah—I'm sorry. That's all I should say. I'm sorry."

"Andi," Noah says with a small smile, "I think I'm the one who's supposed to be apologising, not you. And if anyone should be feeling awkward, it's me, knowing what you overheard."

"Yes, well, I didn't really hear … Okay, I heard everything."

"Exactly. I'm sorry."

"Why? Maybe I …" *Maybe I liked what I overheard. Maybe I liked hearing that you're finally over Tania—whoever she is—and suggesting that I'm the reason you're over her.*

"Maybe you what?" Noah asks.

"Nothing." Heat climbs up my neck and scorches my face. I press my hands over my cheeks. "Sometimes I hate having super pale skin," I murmur.

"Because it means you can never hide it when you're blushing?"

"Yes, Noah, thank you for pointing out the obvious."

"Sure. And since we're still in the middle of a gigantic awkward moment, I'll make it worse by asking how you and Damien are doing."

I press my hands harder against my cheeks. "There is no me and Damien. I don't know if we'll ever even be friends again. What about you guys? Have you made up yet?"

Noah shakes his head. "I think he's still avoiding me. I've tried calling him a few times, but he never answers. I almost called you too. I saw a girl on campus with a handbag made from an actual hardcover book, and I wanted to tell you about it. Looked like something you'd love to make."

I drop my hands to my sides. I'm still standing, he's still standing, and the couch is still between us. And suddenly it seems silly. "I missed you," I say simply, then smack my hand against my forehead. "Ugh, isn't there supposed to be something in my brain that stops things like that from reaching my mouth before I can assess whether they're appropriate or not?"

Noah smiles. "I missed you too."

I laugh, feeling a whole lot better all of a sudden. "Can we sit now? I think this standing thing is adding to the awkwardness."

He walks around the couch and sits down, leaving a free cushion between us. "Are we friends again now?" he asks. "You know, just so I can keep my sister updated. She's been pestering me for details."

Friends? I kinda got the impression he wanted more than that when he was yelling at Damien, but I suppose it isn't an option if he's hoping to restore the friendship he and Damien had. Isn't there a bro code or something? Don't date your friend's ex-girlfriend? And Damien and I should probably try to get back to being friends too. Besides, I told Noah he wasn't my type, didn't I? "So, you told your sister about the fight, did you?" I say.

"Well, she wanted to know when you were visiting again. I said you couldn't, and she wouldn't believe me until I gave her a legitimate reason. Now she keeps asking if I've apologised yet."

"Well, at least now you can legitimately say yes."

"Yes. And explain to her once again that you are just a friend."

"Right." It's surprising how much it disappoints me to hear him say that. I wasn't even aware I wanted more with Noah until the possibility of having more was taken away. When I look back, though, it makes sense. There was a slow progression of Damien-thoughts gradually slipping away and Noah-thoughts taking their place. He's the one who occupies my mind most of the time now, and that isn't normal for someone who's just a friend, is it? Damn, why couldn't I have figured this out weeks ago before I messed everything up?

Noah tilts his head to the side and says, "I'm pretty sure you're my first friend who's a girl."

"Oh." I tuck my hair self-consciously behind my ear. "I guess that's why your family was suspicious when you took me home for dinner."

"They're a suspicious lot, my family."

"Hmm."

"What?"

"I'm just remembering one of my mom's favourite movies, *When Harry Met Sally*."

Noah gives me a blank look. "Never heard of it."

"Yeah, I didn't think you would have. It's quite old, and definitely more of a girl movie than a guy movie."

"And you were thinking of it because …"

"Well, in the movie Billy Crystal says to Meg Ryan that men and women can never be friends because the sex part always gets in the way."

"The—okay." Noah's eyebrows jump before he stares intently at his feet, and suddenly I'm feeling even more awkward than before because I've just suggested that he and I can't be friends because he'll want sex.

"But then," I rush on as heat engulfs my face, "after many years, their characters end up becoming very good friends."

"Ah. So Billy Crystal was wrong." Noah looks relieved.

"Well, then the two of them end up getting married." Aaand now I wish I'd said nothing. And I wish I wasn't staring at his lips. And I wish I wasn't wishing I could kiss him. "I'm sorry," I blurt out, tearing my gaze away from his mouth. "You said I'm your first friend who's a girl, and that made me think of the movie, and I didn't mean to imply that there was ANY kind of similarity between their situation and ours, because of course we—"

"No, I don't think I have any," Livi says as she opens her bedroom door. Noah and I both twist around to see what's happening. I don't know about him, but I'm certainly grateful for the interruption. "I think I've only got herbal teas," Livi continues, "but I'll check."

"I'll help you," Allegra says, following Livi out of her bedroom. "Oh, hello." She gives Noah a flirtatious smile, and I immediately feel a lot less friendly towards her.

Noah and I sit in awkward silence as Livi bustles around making hot drinks. "Do you guys want anything?" she asks us.

Crap, I didn't offer him anything! I'm about to apologise, but he says, "No thanks, I'm fine."

After another minute or so of awkwardness, Allegra leans against the kitchen table and says, "You know, there are few men who can successfully pull off the bald look, but I have to say, you are one of them."

"Uh, thanks," Noah says uncertainly, rubbing a hand over his head.

"He isn't actually bald," I say, feeling oddly defensive. "He does have some hair."

"Yeah." Allegra gives him a sultry half-smile. "A sexy number 1."

"Okay," Livi says, grabbing Allegra's arm and leading her back to the bedroom. "Time to get back to work."

The door closes, and I shut my eyes and sigh. "This evening keeps getting more and more awkward," I mutter.

"Well, thank goodness you're wearing Wonder Woman pyjamas," Noah says, his lips twitching as he attempts to suppress a smile. "That must make everything better, right?"

ON THE FIRST DAY OF THE SECOND QUARTER, AFTER classes are finished, I drag my suitcase back into Fuller. On my second trip back from the car—to fetch my sewing machine and a few other bits and pieces—I see Charlotte leaning in the doorway of the main Fuller entrance. I'm starting to wonder if she stuck a tracking device on me the first day we met; I can't seem to move anywhere in this residence without 'accidentally' running into her.

"Oh, look who's come out of hiding," she says as I walk towards her. "It must have been so embarrassing when your boyfriend dumped you. Not all of us are able to hold our heads high at the end of a relationship."

"And it seems you've once again got the wrong end of the stick," I mutter as I pass her.

"And you're once again wearing circus clothes," Charlotte says, probably referring to my rainbow ruffled skirt and diamond patterned leggings.

I turn around and place my sewing machine on the floor of the foyer. "Look, Charlotte, can we just put an end to this? You're always so spiteful whenever you see me, and I can't say that I enjoy your comments, so I get the feeling we'd both be a lot happier if this game we keep playing could just end."

"This isn't a game, Andi. This is your life, and these are my comments on it. It isn't my fault you've made life choices that are practically begging to be made fun of."

I breathe slowly and deeply in an attempt to remain calm. "I understand why you're upset, Charlotte. You thought your boyfriend was cheating on you, and that must have really hurt—and, honestly, I think you might have been right, although it wasn't with me, and I never got him to admit who the girl was. But it's all in the past now, whether he cheated on you or not, and I think life would be better for us both if we simply ignored each other from now on." I pick up the sewing machine. "That's what I plan to do. It would be great if you could do the same."

As the days pass, I settle into a new kind of normal. Carmen and I hang out most evenings, I see Livi on weekends, and the only time I visit Smuts is if I'm meeting Noah in the foyer. He accompanies me to a new coffee shop each week, and even features in several of the coffee shop videos—

much to the delight of my subscribers. After doing three book reviews together and receiving way too many comments about our relationship status, I buy a plain T-shirt for each of us and whip out my fattest permanent marker. *He is not my boyfriend* goes on my T-shirt, and *She is not my girlfriend* goes on Noah's. My subscribers love it.

Carmen wants to know what all the fuss is about, so I decide to feature her in one of the videos. She doesn't smile and manages to look utterly bored the entire time, only opening her mouth to say things like, "If the bad guys wanted to destroy the stone, why did they follow the good guys all the way to the end and *then* fight them. Why not just fight them as soon as they found them?" and "That's never going to work. You can't have the hero kill the heroine's family, even accidentally. She'll never forgive him. That's the start of a very unhealthy relationship." I'm a little nervous about posting the video, but even those who don't agree with her seem to like her. Carmen's favourite comment is: **Your new friend totally did not get that book. She's a psycho. And she's awesome.**

I run into Damien every now and then, in the dining hall or the corridor or the parking lot. We attempt to make conversation, but it always feels forced. I begin to wonder if we had one of those friendships that was only meant to last our school years. Sometimes it hurts to think of that, and other times I wonder why it matters if each of us has clearly moved in a different direction now. Noah manages to make more progress than I do, but he says Damien is distant with him as well, and neither of them shares anything too personal with the other. Damien's mentioned a new girlfriend, apparently, but he won't say much about her.

And that's how I know I've truly moved on. The thought of Damien's new girlfriend doesn't fill me with hurt or jealousy or disappointment. It fills me with excitement—because if Damien's moved on, then maybe I'm finally allowed a chance with the guy I've been falling a little more for every day.

"So to summarise," I say to the camera, "we have finally found a book that Noah thinks is awesome and I don't really like that much."

"Probably because there's barely any romance in it," Noah says, leaning back on his hands.

"Well, exactly. What is a hero meant to fight for if not love?"

"Uh, the fate of his kingdom?"

"Yes, I know, I know. The dragons were going to kill them all, and he wanted to keep his darling princess safe, so he left her back at the castle, and that's pretty much the last we saw of her. But instead we could have had a princess with a little more guts. She could have escaped the castle and gone into dragon territory on her own. And let's say some of those dragons were good and didn't actually want to attack the kingdom. She could have befriended one of them and gone back with it to her kingdom to share secrets that could help her people win. She could have been a *dragon rider!* And then, at the turning point of the battle, she could almost die—or the hero could almost die—and then there would be that heartbreaking moment when the dragon sacrifices himself for his rider, and the prince and princess get to live happily ever after in a kingdom no longer under threat."

I look at Noah. He stares at me with an odd half-smile lingering on his lips. I stare back. "What?" I ask.

"Nothing."

I narrow my eyes at him, then look back at the camera. "Is it just me, or is he giving me a weird look?"

"It's just you," Noah says. "And the fact that your version of the story sucks."

"Hey, my version definitely does not—"

"And that's all we have time for today," Noah says loudly, reaching over me for the remote and pinning me down so I can't take it away from him. I fight to get him off me, but I don't put a great deal of effort into it because he's half on top of me, and—let's be honest—why would I want that to stop? "And I won't be replying to comments over the next few days," Noah adds, still speaking to the camera, "as I'll be away working on a Habitat for Humanity project. Andi has all the time in the world to reply to you, though. Harass her if she doesn't. See you on the other side!" He ends the recording and rolls away from me. "Sorry," he says, laughing. "I didn't mean to squash you."

I almost reach out and pull him back. I could still do it. He's right there. I could tug him down and kiss him, and maybe—just maybe—he'd kiss me back.

"Andi?"

"Mmm? Yeah?"

"I think you zoned out for a second."

"Oh. Um. The Habitat for Humanity project. Remind me how long you're away for?"

"Four nights." Noah climbs off the bed, pulls off his jacket—doesn't he *ever* get cold?—and removes the memory card from the camera. "It's further away than some of the other projects I've been involved in, so we're gonna stay over there instead of driving back each day."

"Oh, okay." Four days without seeing Noah. Is it going to be as excruciating as I imagine it will?

"I have an idea," he says. He returns to the bed and leans over me. He lowers his voice and says, "I dare you to upload this video without looking at it."

I remind myself to breathe—because apparently my body has forgotten how to do that on its own—and say, "Um, why?"

He shrugs. "Because I dared you to."

"But what if there's something that needs to be cut out? A pause that's too long, or a moment where I rambled too much."

"It'll be fine. You don't need to cut anything."

I narrow my eyes at him. "Why do I get the feeling you did something I don't know about?"

He smiles. "Do you trust me?"

Is he speaking about the video now, or something else? Perhaps I'm reading more into it than I should, but his words make me think of all the shouting Damien and I did about lies and deception and faking, and I know that Noah isn't like that. "Yes," I whisper.

"Okay." He stands up and reaches for my hand. "Then you can upload it without taking all that time to check and tweak the whole thing."

I take his hand and let him pull me up. I want to hold onto him, but his hand is gone the moment I'm standing. "But I still need to add the intro video and the end bit."

"Sure, okay, but you can do that without looking through the whole of the middle section, can't you?"

"I suppose." I take the memory card from him and sit at my desk. I plug it in, copy the video across, and open it in the relevant software. "Oh, you can turn the light off now that we're done recording," I say to Noah. The harsh light disappears a moment later, and we're left with the warm glow of fairy lights and the lamp on my desk.

I quickly add the standard extra bits of video to the beginning and end of our book review while Noah tidies up my bed. I'm tempted to drag the cursor quickly across the video to see if he did something I wasn't aware of, but I'm pretty sure he's paying attention to every click I make right now, despite his cushion-rearranging act.

"Hey, have you spoken to Damien lately?" I ask. "I was wondering how he feels about you and me hanging out a lot. He should be okay with it, right, considering he has a new girlfriend?"

"I don't actually know," Noah says. "He shies away from conflict and confrontation—"

"Except for that one gigantic fight."

"Except for that, which he didn't initiate, so I don't know how he feels about you and me hanging out."

I swivel my chair so I'm facing Noah. "You know, I never noticed that before about him avoiding conflict and confrontation, but you're right. That must be why he and I never fought. If I happened to disagree with him about something, he'd simply change the subject. Do you think that's why he ends every relationship when it hits a bump? He'd rather move on than deal with whatever the problem is?"

"Maybe," Noah says. "But he's never spoken to me much about his relationships, so I don't know."

"Hmm." I turn back to my desk. "Okay, this is done. I'll upload it now."

"Great." He leans his hip against the desk. "See how fast it goes when you don't have to check every frame of the video? I just created more reading time for you. You can thank me later."

"Uh huh." I smile as I click my way around YouTube. "I'll wait to see if you've done anything embarrassing on this video. If not, *then* I'll thank you for all the extra reading time."

"Deal. Oh, are these the new bracelets you told me about?"

"Hmm?" I finish filling in all the video details, then push the laptop out of the way so the video can finish uploading on its own. "Yes." I wheel my chair back and stand. I lean past Noah—is my excuse to brush against his arm as obvious as I think it is?—and pull the container of bracelets closer. "Paper beads. Strips cut from the pages of books, rolled up and varnished. I made a whole lot this afternoon."

"Did you make one for yourself?"

"Oh, well, not specifically, but any one of them could be mine."

"How about this one?" Noah says, removing a bracelet from the pile. "I see the name Darcy on it, which means it'll go perfectly with your *I ♥ Mr Darcy* badge. A badge you'll have to stop wearing when you eventually get a boyfriend."

"Oh," I say with a smile, "do you think my boyfriend will have a problem with my love of *Pride and Prejudice*?"

"No, of course not." Noah reaches for my right arm and slowly lifts it. My traitorous heart speeds up immediately and my lungs forget to breathe again. "He may have a problem with your love of Mr Darcy, though." He pushes my sleeve back, almost to my elbow, and slips the bracelet over my hand and onto my wrist.

Holy smoking sexiness ... I go from not breathing to breathing way too fast.

Instead of releasing my hand, he slides his fingers between mine. A shiver runs up my arm and across my neck. Blood pumps loudly in my ears, and I'm too scared to look up and find his eyes. I love the way his skin looks next to mine. Deeply tanned against palest white.

I dare to let my gaze slide slowly up his chest, over the words *She is not my girlfriend,* stopping at the tattoo peeking out below the T-shirt sleeve on his right arm. I lift my free hand and trace an almost-trembling finger over the outline of the bird. I hear him breathe in—sharper than normal—and it gives me the courage to look up.

His gaze is uncertain, questioning, and his lips—those beautiful, full lips I've dreamed of kissing—are parted. He tilts his head forwards and down. I lean closer to him, my fingers tightening around his. My eyes close as another shiver spreads from my neck down my spine and across my arms. His lips touch mine—

"Andi?" *Knock, knock, knock.* "Andi, are you there?"

Startled, I step back, bumping my chair, which hits the desk.

"Who—" Noah says, but I hastily place two fingers over his lips. I stare unblinking into his eyes, silently willing Carmen to leave. Noah's burning gaze never leaves mine. I can feel his breath against my hand, his soft lips against my fingers.

"Andi, please ..." Carmen says. Her voice is so much quieter than usual. Quieter and distressed.

I drop my hand and hurry across the room. Unlocking and pulling open the door, I say, "Carmen? What's wrong?"

"It's ..." She closes her eyes and tears run down her cheeks. "My mom just called us. Grandpa ... passed away just now."

I pull her towards me and hug her. "Oh, I'm so sorry." Over her shoulder, I see her cousin Tania sitting at the top of the stairs, her head on her arms.

"It's just ... I know he was old and it was obviously his time to go," Carmen says tearfully into my ear, "but it's still really sad because he was such a big part of our lives. He's been there for everything. Now he'll never see me graduate or get married or … any of that."

I hear Noah's footsteps behind me. "I'm really sorry, Carmen," he says quietly, reaching over me and patting her shoulder.

Tania looks up. Her eyebrows pull together sharply. "*Ferry?*" She jumps to her feet. "What the hell are you doing here?"

Carmen pulls out of my embrace and backs away from me, her eyes on Noah. "You're Noah *Ferreira?*" she demands. Her face morphs from shock to anger. "I *knew* you looked familiar."

"Tania, I'm sorry," Noah says, slowly walking past me onto the landing. "I didn't know Carmen was your cousin. I'm not here to upset you, and I'm really sorry about your grandfather—"

"*Moenie waag om oor my oupa te praat nie,*" Tania yells. "*Jy het sy kleinseun van hom af weggeneem. Jy't sy hart gebreek nes jy myne gebreek het en almal in ons familie s'n.*"

"Tania," Noah says, raising his hands slightly, "*dit was 'n ongeluk.*"

"*Nee!*" She rushes at him and starts beating her fists against his chest. "*Dit was jou skuld en ek haat jou. Ek haat jou want jy het hom van ons af weggeneem!*"

Carmen pulls Tania away from Noah and wraps her arms around her. "Get the hell out of here," she growls at Noah.

"I'm sorry," he mutters, then walks past them, his head down, towards the stairs.

"Noah?" I call after him, but he refuses to look back at me. He hurries down the stairs, his footsteps growing quieter as Tania's sobs grow louder. "What just happened?" I ask.

"That was him," Carmen says, her eyes red and glassy with unshed tears. "The one who was in the car accident with Tyrone. He got Tyrone drunk and let him drive. Then they crashed and Tyrone didn't make it. Noah's the reason Tyrone is dead."

28

IT'S LATE WHEN I WALK OUT OF FULLER WITH A BLANKET wrapped around me. Tania's friend came to fetch her and drive her home, and Carmen gave me another speech about what an awful person Noah Ferreira is. Then I went to bed with all that information buzzing around my head, even though I knew the chance of finding sleep would be slim.

So I make my way to mem stone, the place I always go to when I need to think. As I approach it, I stare at the letters on the side of the stone. IN MEMORIAM, 1914 - 1918, 1939 - 1945. I've seen the words before, of course, but I've never thought about them. Never thought about what this stone actually represents. I've walked past it hundreds of times, sat on it many nights while contemplating my trivial life problems, but I've never realised that this is a memorial to the people who died in world wars.

I climb carefully on top of it, as if I need to be more

reverent now that I know its real meaning. I run my hand gently over the cold stone top. I suppose it's fitting to be here on a night when all I can think about are people who've died. Carmen's grandfather and Noah's friend. Was it really Noah's fault that he died? Or is there more to the story?

"Andi." I look over my shoulder and see Noah walking towards me in tracksuit pants and a hoodie. "Thanks for your message."

I look forwards as he raises himself onto the stone beside me. We sit in silence while I wait for him to talk. He knows that's why we're here. It's his chance to explain his side of events.

"I was a different person back then," he says eventually. "I was just like Damien at school. Hard-working, responsible, earned myself a bursary. Then I got here and it felt like I was finally free of all the pressure. Like I could finally relax and enjoy life instead of just study, study, study. Life was great. Tyrone had been my best friend since we started high school, and Tania, his sister, had been my girlfriend almost as long. I thought I'd marry her one day.

"We partied a lot, Tyrone and I. We drank a lot. We experimented with … just about everything. Tyrone managed to keep most of it secret from his family, but Tania knew. She kept telling me to stop being a bad influence on her brother. I don't think she realised it was Tyrone who always found the next party. Tyrone who always said, 'Let's just have one more.'

"The night of the accident, Tyrone was driving my car.

We'd both had too much to drink, but I was way worse, so he took the keys from me. I was too out of it to remember much, but I was told afterwards that it was a red light, and Tyrone didn't stop, and a truck hit the driver's side of the car.

"I woke up in the hospital a day later to the news that my best friend was dead. Tania came in after my family left and told me if I ever went near her family again, she'd kill me." Noah rubs a hand over his face and takes a deep breath. "I haven't touched a drop of alcohol since that night. I stopped going to places where I knew I'd be tempted to drink. My friendships with those who enjoyed the party life soon fell away, but my friends who'd never been big into the party scene—friends like Damien and Yashen—stuck around. I managed to scrape through my exams at the end of that first semester, and after that, things got easier. I worked harder, I got involved in social development projects, and I honoured Tania's request to never go near her or her family again.

"I still think of Tyrone, of course. I think of how different life might be if that night had never happened. I think of everything I could have done to prevent the accident. But … those kinds of thoughts are torture. I try to stay away from them.

"So." He pushes his hands into the front pocket of his hoodie. "That's what happened. That's why Tania and Carmen hate me."

We sit for a while in silence as my mind runs over everything he said. "Why didn't you tell me before?" I ask eventually.

"Well … partly because you made it clear that you think private lives should remain private, so—"

"Wait, I said that in a moment of extreme anger. You know I don't feel that way anymore, so don't make it my fault that you didn't say anything."

"And the other part," Noah continues, "is that … I didn't want it to change the way you see me. I've let so many people down. All the things I've done wrong … they're always following me around like shadows I can never get rid of. I've changed, and no one speaks about the person I used to be, but everyone knows. Everyone remembers. Everyone except you. You could see me simply for who I am now and not for who I used to be."

I lean forwards and place my head in my hands, not knowing how to respond to him. Does my opinion of him matter so much that he'd keep this from me? Is that the truth? Is any of what he's told me tonight the truth? "Noah, I … I can't even begin to imagine what you've been through. And this does change how I see you, but not in the way you think. It doesn't make me think less of you. It makes you … more *real* to me."

He breathes out a sigh that sounds relieved. "That's all I wanted. I just wanted us to be real. I pushed and pushed until eventually you were real with me, and only then did I realise how scared I was to be real with you. I wanted to tell you everything the night I came to see you at your sister's flat. I wanted to get everything out so we could start afresh. I figured you were already angry with me at that point, so how much worse could I make it? But then … things went well that night, and we were laughing and getting along, and I couldn't bring myself to ruin that.

"And then tonight, after the video, I was planning to bring it up, but then … I let myself get distracted. And then Tania was there and it came out anyway, but it was so much worse than if I'd told you myself. As if God were saying, 'Well, I've given you enough chances and you haven't told her, so I'm putting it in someone else's hands to tell her instead.' And I couldn't look at you because I was afraid to see how angry you were."

"I wasn't angry. I was … confused."

Noah looks up. "And are you angry now?"

I look down at my hands. At my fingers that, not many hours ago, were entwined with his. "I don't know what I am," I murmur.

Noah looks away from me and out over the city. "Okay."

"It's just that earlier tonight, you asked me if I trust you. I said yes, and I meant it. But now I have no idea what else you might be hiding."

He turns to face me. "This is me, Andi." He spreads his hands out, palms up. "The real me. The ugly bits and the good bits. There's nothing left to hide."

I nod slowly. "Maybe … maybe we just need some time. Because right now I don't know how to trust you."

29

I SLEEP THROUGH MY ALARM THE NEXT MORNING AND wake up ten minutes before my first lecture begins. "Crap," I mumble, dropping my phone back onto the desk. I lie in bed for another few minutes, listening to the rain outside—*don't think about Noah*—then force myself out of bed. I shuffle out to the landing—*don't think about Noah*—find a small tub of yoghurt in the fridge Carmen and I share, and sit on the edge of my bed while eating it and staring at the paper heart on my pinboard. Not the one from Damien. I pulled that off and threw it away weeks ago. I'm staring at the one from—

Don't think about Noah.

But I can't focus on anything else. He's there all the time, in every thought that passes through my mind. The coffee shop visits—

Best French toast in the world.

—the afternoon I watched him play Savage Time with his young cousins—

Whatever the rules are, it generally ends up with all four of them attacking each other in a heap on the ground.

—the moment he saw right through me—

So essentially … this heroine is you.

—the day he confronted me about my mother—

Life isn't perfect, and that's okay.

—the night he came to Livi's to apologise—

If anyone should be feeling awkward, it's me, knowing what you overheard.

—his story last night—

I woke up in the hospital a day later to the news that my best friend was dead.

It hits me suddenly. A pain in my chest. A pain that comes with the realisation that *I love him* and instead of telling him that, instead of pulling him into my arms and comforting him after that horrific story about his friend's death, my last words to him were, 'I don't know how to trust you.'

I toss the empty yoghurt tub into my bin, hurry to the bathroom, and brush my teeth. I think Noah may have left already, but I'll stop at Smuts on the way to my next lecture just in case. I rush back to my room, pick up my phone to check the time—and only then do I see all the emails notifying me of the comments on the YouTube video I uploaded last night. I almost ignore them and carry on getting ready, but the most recent one says, **Have you seen this yet, Andi? We're dying here waiting for your response!!!**

"What?" I murmur.

There are so many emails that instead of opening each one, I go straight to the video itself to read the comments.

Apple Turtle (21 min ago)
Have you seen this yet, Andi? We're dying here waiting for your response!!!

Minny J (35 min ago)
Yes! #CrossOutTheNot

JanACE (1 hour ago)
Eeeeeeeeek! So much romantic, love it!

> **Apple Turtle** (19 min ago)
> I know! So romantic! *Sighs*

Mandy Lovet (1 hour ago)
Cutest thing I've seen on YouTube in ages :)

LollyMBooks (1 hour ago)
OMG Noah! Heart you!

NL Winters (2 hours ago)
I'm totally tweeting this! #CrossOutTheNot

Minny J (3 hours ago)
We've been dying for you to cross out the 'not' for weeks ;-)

There are many more comments, but I scroll back up to

the video so I can see what they're all talking about. I switch my phone off silent and hit the play button. The video begins with me showing off the book Noah and I are about to talk about. Nothing weird so far. Noah blabbers on about the terrific fight scenes, I let everyone know how boring I thought they were, and still there's nothing strange going on.

"So to summarise," video-me says, "we have finally found a book that Noah thinks is awesome and I don't really like that much."

"Probably because there's barely any romance in it," Noah says. He leans back on his hands, but then he lifts one hand up behind my head, and in it is an A4 piece of card with writing on it: **ANDI AGREED TO UPLOAD THIS VIDEO WITHOUT WATCHING IT FIRST.**

A shiver races from the top of my spine down along my arms. What is this? And how did he know I would agree to that?

"Well, exactly," video-me says. "What is a hero meant to fight for if not love?"

Noah's hand rises behind my head again with a card that reads **SHE HAS NO IDEA THESE SIGNS ARE GOING UP BEHIND HER HEAD.** "Uh, the fate of his kingdom?"

"Yes, I know, I know. The dragons were going to kill them all, and he wanted to keep his darling princess safe, so he left her back at the castle, and that's pretty much the last we saw of her."

ANDI, I'M FALLING IN LOVE WITH YOU.

At the sight of the third sign, my shaking thumb hits pause.

I'm falling in love with you.

I'm falling in love with you.

Yes, I definitely read that correctly. I press a hand over my mouth and touch the play symbol again.

"But instead we could have had a princess with a little more guts," video-me continues.

I'VE SPENT THE PAST FEW YEARS UNABLE TO FORGET THE DEMONS OF MY PAST.

"She could have escaped the castle and gone into dragon territory on her own."

BUT YOU'VE REMINDED ME WHAT IT IS TO BE HAPPY.

"And let's say some of those dragons were good and didn't actually want to attack the kingdom."

ON THE SURFACE WE LOOK LIKE WE COULD NEVER SUIT EACH OTHER.

"She could have befriended one of them and gone back with it to her kingdom to share secrets that could help her people win. She could have been a *dragon rider!*"

BUT I KNOW THE REAL YOU, AND THE REAL YOU IS PERFECT FOR THE REAL ME.

"And then, at the turning point of the battle, she could almost die—or the hero could almost die—and then there would be that heartbreaking moment when the dragon sacrifices himself for his rider, and the prince and princess get to live happily ever after in a kingdom no longer under threat."

I WANT TO BE WITH YOU. PLEASE SAY YES SO WE CAN CROSS OUT THE 'NOT.'

"Cross out the 'not,'" I murmur, dropping the phone on

my bed as it finally makes sense. I grab the *He is not my boyfriend* T-shirt from the back of my chair, reach for my permanent marker, and draw a line firmly through the 'not.' Pyjama top off, find bra, pull on T-shirt, zip up jacket. Lastly, I replace my slippers with gumboots and grab my keys as I run out the room.

I splash my way across the parking lot, earning myself a number of odd looks from other students. *What?* I want to say to them. *Don't you ever wear your pyjama pants on campus?* Two guys are leaving Smuts as I get there, which means I run right through. Along the corridor, up the stairs, up some more stairs—Noah chose to live on the top floor of his flat—and finally I'm in front of the right door. My boot makes a weird noise when I walk, and I look down and find a piece of paper stuck beneath it. I bend down and, removing it, find that it's a flyer for the Smuts formal. I fold it up, put it in my pocket, and knock on Noah's door.

Please be here, please be here, please be—

The door opens. "Andi." Noah's face lights up. "I thought … I thought you said you needed some time. I didn't think I'd see you until after—"

"I got your message," I say breathlessly.

"My message?"

I unzip my jacket and let it slide off. He looks startled for a second—probably due to me undressing myself in his doorway—but a smile grows slowly on his face as he reads my T-shirt. He pulls me inside the room and shuts the door.

"I'm sorry I said I didn't know how to trust you last night," I say.

"Andi, you—"

"I realised that I do. And if I could go back, I'd say something completely different. I'd say that I love you no matter what mistakes you've made. And I don't need any time. I love you now, and I want to be with you now, and I—"

He takes my face in both his hands and kisses me. I stand on tiptoe and wind my arms around his neck, kissing him back with all the longing that's been building inside me over the past weeks. His hands slide around my thighs, and he lifts me easily. I wrap my legs around his waist, but with my gumboots on, I end up kicking him.

"Oh, crap, sorry," I say through my laughter. "Stupid boots."

He swings me around and drops me onto the bed, then pulls each boot off. "Not a problem anymore," he says with a grin. He crawls onto the bed until he's half next to me and half over me. I slip my hands around his neck and pull him closer. His lips—as soft as I imagined them—meet mine. Warmth swells in my chest and my pulse quickens. His hand slides over my bare arm, my waist, my hip, down the side of my leg. When he reaches the crook of my knee, he pulls my leg up and over his. I arch against him, tasting his tongue and feeling his breath and wanting more, more, more.

His phone rings. "No," he mumbles against my lips. "That's my lift."

"Don't go," I whisper. I run my hands over his short hair, something I've been longing to do for ages.

"I wish I didn't have to."

I open my eyes and find his—beautiful gold-brown bleeding into grey-green—right there. I wonder if my gaze is burning with the fire I feel inside. I feel shy all of a sudden with him so close, as if he can see right into my soul. I almost look away, but I manage to hold his gaze. I trace my finger gently over the scar above his left eyebrow. "Was this from the car accident?"

He nods. "A reminder every time I look in the mirror of how I messed up."

"We've all messed up, Noah. We all make mistakes. You're the one who reminded me of that."

"Some mistakes are bigger than others."

"That doesn't mean you have to keep silently beating yourself up about it. It's in the past. You've dealt with it. You're not that person anymore."

With a smile on his lips, he whispers, "I think I love you." The word 'love' sends a thrill racing through my body, lighting up the fire inside me once more. But perhaps he takes my lack of response as a bad sign, because he adds, "Sorry. Too soon?"

I shake my head against the pillow. "You already said it during your secret slideshow in the video."

He places a kiss on my neck. "And you said it when you walked in here just now."

I tilt my head and find his lips and kiss them once more. "I wish you didn't have to go," I whisper.

His hands frame my face. "It's only four days," he says with a gentle smile.

"I know, but two of them are Saturday and Sunday, and

they're going to take sooooo long to pass."

He kisses me again, long and lingering. When he breaks away and sits up, he says, "Walk outside with me. I want to introduce my beautiful new girlfriend to the guys I'll be working with for the next few days."

"Um, in this?" I sit up and gesture to my pyjama pants and gumboots.

"You look gorgeous," he says. "You could be wearing a tea cosy on your head, and I'd still want to show you off to everyone."

I pull my boots back on—with Noah's help, which he manages to do in a way that's so sexy I almost tug him back onto the bed—and zip my jacket up over my *He is not my boyfriend* T-shirt. Noah picks up a duffle bag, slings the strap over his shoulder, and slips his hand around mine. He gives me another quick kiss before we walk down to reception and out to the parking lot where, fortunately, it's stopped raining, and two guys are waiting by a car.

"Taking your time, Ferreira," one of them says, but despite his attempt to look annoyed, I see the smile in his eyes.

"I think we all know why," the other one says, grinning at the first guy.

They greet each other, and Noah introduces me. He throws his duffle bag onto the back seat of the car, then takes my hand and pulls me aside. He wraps his arms around me and kisses my forehead.

"Can I say one more thing before you go?" I ask.

He nods, kisses my lips, and says, "Of course."

"Remember Valentine's Day? When I turned down that opportunity to dance with you and you said I'd regret it one day?"

"Yip."

"I think I'm regretting it now."

"I see."

"And I think there might be a way you could help me out with that."

"Oh really?"

I nod and open my hand to reveal the folded-up flyer I stuffed into my pocket just now.

"Hmm." He takes it from me. He must recognise what it is from the colours, because he doesn't bother unfolding it. "You know, I never did get an answer to the message on that heart I gave you."

I think of the paper heart stuck to my pinboard. *Be my valentine.* I wrap my arms around his neck, stand on tiptoe, and whisper in his ear, "I would love to be your valentine."

"In that case—" he kisses my earlobe "—Andrea Clark, would you like to go to the Smuts formal with me?"

I'M STILL PUTTING THE FINISHING TOUCHES TO MY OUTFIT when there's a knock on my door. *Shoot!* What is he doing here? He's got to be at least forty minutes early.

"Relax," Carmen says from the other side of my door. "It's just me."

I pad across the room in my slippers and open the door. Carmen's standing on the other side looking glamorous and model-like in a long, close-fitting red gown. "Oh, wow, you look amazing."

"Yeah, yeah, whatever."

Okay, then. "Um, have you had a chance to think about what I said yesterday?"

"You mean what you *yelled* yesterday?"

"Uh, yes." Carmen and I have spent all week fighting about Noah—she still thinks he's a terrible person, while I've been trying to convince her otherwise—until yesterday when I shouted, 'Noah did *not* kill your cousin. And even if he was this terrible, evil influence you seem to think he is, Tyrone was his friend and I highly doubt he *forced* him to do anything. Tyrone *chose* to drink that night. He *chose* to get behind the wheel of a car. And he *chose* not to stop at a red light. End of story. If you want to hate Noah for the decisions Tyrone made, go right ahead. That's your illogical business, not mine.'

"Well, you know I'm a very practical, stick-to-the-facts kinda person," Carmen says, placing a hand on her hip, "so I didn't just think about what you said. I did some research."

"Research?"

"I hunted down some of Ty's friends from back then and asked them a few questions."

I smile because I can imagine Carmen hunting people down. Literally.

"Despite the fact that Tania has always insisted her brother was a good guy who never chose to get involved in any of that stuff—drinking and drugs and all that—the friends he used to have said he was always, well, the life of the party. That he was excited when his uptight younger cousin Noah left school and decided to relax and join in the fun. So I guess it wasn't Noah who led Ty off the tracks. If anything, it was the other way around."

Relief warms my insides. "Carmen, that's—"

"And while this does not mean that I have to *like* Noah," Carmen says, holding a finger up, "I do now see that it's illogical to blame him for Ty's death."

I smile. "Thank you."

"And don't expect me say that again. You know how I feel about admitting that I'm wrong."

"I do." I watch in amusement as she sashays back to her room. She wasn't entirely sure about this whole formal thing, but one of the few Smuts guys who isn't afraid of her asked her to go with him, and, after making him wait several days for an answer, she said yes.

I spend the next forty minutes finishing my make-up and hair. I'm lacing up my boots when Noah knocks on my door. I know it's him—I recognise the way he knocks—and my stomach fills with anxious butterflies. Will he like what I'm wearing? Will he think I'm pretty? Will he be embarrassed to be seen with me?

With a shy smile on my face, I pull open the door. Noah looks dashing in a suit, completely different from his normal casual attire. At the sight of me, his eyes widen. "Wow," he says. "Just ... wow."

I'm wearing my version of a steampunk dress. The centrepiece of the outfit is a Victorian-style coat, tight at the waist and flaring out like a skirt over my hips. I added a few ruffled layers, longer at the back and shorter at the front, to fill out the skirt. Under that I've got black stockings and high-heeled ankle boots—visible from the front where the skirt is shorter. Brass buttons shaped like cogs add to the steampunk look of the coat-dress, along with the old pocket watch I hung on a short chain so it sits against the V of bare skin beneath my neck. Lastly, I twisted my hair up and pinned a tiny top hat to the side of the twist.

"Is that a good 'wow'?" I ask.

"Yes. That is a my-girlfriend-is-the-sexiest-and-most-beautiful-thing-I've-ever-seen wow."

I reach for his hand as a blush rises in my cheeks. "I like that kinda wow." I lean forward and whisper, "I thought you were sexy enough in normal clothes, but you're even sexier in a suit."

Smiling, he raises my hand and kisses it. "I'd prefer to kiss your lips," he says, "but I don't want to ruin your make-up."

"Hmm. Maybe I don't mind having my make-up ruined."

He brushes his lips against my cheek. "Don't tempt me."

With a laugh, I step back and look around for my keys. "So, shall we get going?"

"Wait, what about my steampunk accessories?"

I look at him. "Really?"

"Of course. You're my date. We should match."

I tilt my head to the side. "Are you sure?"

"Andi, when it comes to you, I am always sure."

"Oh good," I say, clapping my hands together, "because I got you some stuff, but I didn't know if you'd want to wear it or not. Nothing overboard, of course."

"Of course," Noah says.

I open my cupboard and pull out the items I got for Noah. "Here's a top hat. I stuck a watch face on the side along with a few of the clockwork brass buttons I used on my coat."

"Awesome. I've always wanted to wear a top hot."

"And these cufflinks have watch parts stuck to them, so they're in keeping with the steampunk vibe."

"Perfect."

"Really? I thought maybe you'd think they're stupid or—"

He silences me with a kiss, obviously no longer bothered by my make-up. I melt against him, wondering if perhaps we should give the formal a miss and stay here all night. But he pulls back after a few moments, and I remember that I'm looking forward to showing off my dress and dancing with Noah. "Um, I may need to reapply my lipstick now."

"And I probably need to remove it," he says, ducking out of my room. I hear him turn on the tap in the bathroom.

A few moments later, after adding a quick layer of lipstick, I pull my door shut and meet Noah on the landing. "Ready?" he asks.

"Ready."

Fairy lights glow like stars above us, and beneath us, the polished dance floor gleams. My feet ache from dancing so much, but right here in Noah's arms is exactly where I want to be. So I unlace my boots, toss them to the side of the dance floor, and skip back to Noah on my stockinged feet.

"Steampunk pixie," he says into my ear before spinning me around again.

"Steampunk hunk," I say with a laugh after the spinning ends and he catches me.

It's been a fun evening, with several people complimenting my outfit, and only one person making a rude comment to my face. He suggested I got lost on the way to a theme party, but Noah simply said, "Hey, remember when you fell out of a window?" and the guy backed off pretty quickly.

The music slows, and Noah pulls me closer. I link my arms around his neck. Over his shoulder, I see Damien. He's with a girl whom I assume is his new girlfriend. I wonder for a moment if she's the girl he wrote the letter to. The letter he may or may not have sent. I find, though, that it doesn't matter to me anymore. Maybe he lied and maybe he didn't, but I've moved on.

I rest my cheek against Noah's shoulder, enjoying the feel of his strong arms wrapped around me. We sway slowly, and I rub my thumb gently up and down the back of his neck.

"This is perfect," Noah murmurs.

I lift my head so I can look at him. "I thought you said there's no such thing as perfect."

"There isn't. At least, there aren't any perfect people. But there's a footnote to that statement." He leans his forehead against mine. "Two imperfect people can make a perfect moment."

I close my eyes. It is a perfect moment. Even though the music is cheesy and the food wasn't all that amazing and the hotel ballroom has a musty smell and the stars twinkling above us aren't real, it's still perfect. Because I'm with him.

epilogue

"Hey, guys!" I wave at the camera. "Sorry to make
you wait a WHOLE TWO WEEKS for this announcement,
but after our last book review, Noah went away for four
days—"

"And Andi was too busy missing me to think about
replying to your comments," Noah says.

"And then the Thursday coffee shop video went live
because it was already done and uploaded, and most of you
DISLIKED that video because it wasn't about Noah and
me—"

"Not cool, guys. Not cool." Noah shakes his head,
showing the camera his mock-serious face.

"And then the next Tuesday book review day came
around and …" I look at Noah. He looks at me. He winks,
and I grin stupidly at the memory of last Tuesday's make-
out session. "… and, well, we were otherwise occupied," I

say, facing the camera once more. "Fast forward through another automatic coffee shop video, which was bombarded by #CrossOutTheNot comments, and here we are."

"Thanking ourselves for never making our residential addresses public," Noah adds, "because at least half of you would have hunted us down by now if we had."

"Right. Anyway. Back to that announcement we were talking about."

"Oh yes," Noah says. We look at one another and each reach for the zips of the jackets we're wearing. I take a deep breath and face the camera again. I whip my zip down, revealing my *He is ~~not~~ my boyfriend* T-shirt, at the same time as Noah whips his down, revealing his—naked chest?

"Noah!" I look around for his T-shirt and spot it on my desk chair.

"Oh, jeez, am I supposed to be wearing something under here?" Noah says, giving the camera a confused look. "This is embarrassing. I obviously didn't get the mem—" His balled-up T-shirt hits the side of his head. "Oh, is this what I'm supposed to be wearing?" He pulls off his jacket, giving me—and, before long, the whole of YouTube—an excellent view of his dark, muscular chest and arms. He pulls the T-shirt on, then stands and walks closer to the camera until only the T-shirt is visible. "How about that, ladies and gentlemen? The NOT has officially been CROSSED."

"Woohoo!" I shout from behind him. I grab the T-shirt and pull him back onto the bed. He rolls over and pins me down, out of view of the camera, and places kisses along my neck in a hurried, ticklish trail that makes me giggle uncontrollably.

"Don't mind us," Noah says loudly between kisses. "We're just gonna be busy down here for a little bit."

I push him off me and manage to sit up. I smooth my hands over my hair. "Sorry about that. So, the book we're talking about today is—"

"Seriously?" Noah sits up. "You're actually going to review a book?"

"Yes."

"I don't think anyone's interested in hearing about books today."

"Possibly not, but when you record yourself removing articles of clothing and making out with someone, it no longer qualifies as a book review. In fact, I think it goes in an entirely different category. So just to be safe, I'm going to briefly talk about a book." I reach for *Shifting Stone* and hold it up. "Not my favourite book by this author, but still a great read. In fact, it has what could possibly be the best kissing scene I've read this—"

My back hits the cushions, and I find myself looking up at Noah's mischievous grin. "That's enough book reviewing for today," he says, pointing the remote at the camera and turning off the recording. "But tell me more about this kissing scene."

I take the remote from him and toss it somewhere amongst the cushions behind him. I wrap my legs around his waist and pull him closer. "Well, there's a hot guy."

"Okay." He touches his lips to my palm.

"And the girl he's been dying to kiss since about page ten."

"Mm hmm." His lips graze the crook of my elbow.

"And there's an elevator and water and a collapsing building and a terrifying sphinx-type monster."

"Huh. Sounds just like us, doesn't it?"

I laugh until his lips find mine, and then he kisses me, and the rest of the world melts away.

VISIT

WWW.TROUBLESERIES.COM

FOR BONUS MATERIAL BASED ON
THE TROUBLE WITH FAKING

AND DON'T MISS OUT ON THE REST OF
THE TROUBLE SERIES!

THE TROUBLE
WITH
flying
ROCHELLE MORGAN

THE TROUBLE
WITH
flirting
ROCHELLE MORGAN

THE TROUBLE
WITH
faking
ROCHELLE MORGAN

THE TROUBLE
WITH
falling
ROCHELLE MORGAN

ACKNOWLEDGEMENTS

Thank you, God, for loving me even though I'm far from perfect.

Thank you, Nicola Vermaak, for your valuable insight during the editing phase of this book. You helped Andi and Noah's story come alive, and without you, Noah wouldn't be nearly as hot!

Thank you, Rob Goldman, for coming up with Savage Time. As crazy as it sounds for a neat-freak, afraid-of-the-dirt child, I loved being chased around and dangled upside down over molehills! Those are happy memories.

Thank you to every reader who's passionate enough about books to make booktubing a real thing, and to all the creative geniuses on Etsy. You inspired a large part of Andi's character.

And thank you, Kyle, for being the other imperfect half of our many perfect moments.

Rochelle Morgan is the contemporary romance
pen name of author Rachel Morgan.

Rachel spent a good deal of her childhood living in a
fantasy land of her own making, crafting endless stories of
make-believe and occasionally writing some of them down.
After completing a degree in genetics and discovering
she still wasn't grown-up enough for a 'real' job, she decided
to return to those story worlds still spinning around her
imagination. These days she spends much of her time
immersed in fantasy land once more, writing fiction
for young adults and those young at heart.

Rachel lives in Cape Town with her husband and
three miniature dachshunds.

www.rochellemorganbooks.com